Walking on Edge

A Pilgrimage to Santiago

Reino Gevers

ISBN: 978-0-692-16686-4

DEDICATION

To all pilgrims on an inner and outer journey

Every journey has a secret destination of which
the traveler is unaware

-Martin Buber -

CONTENTS

ACKNOWLEDGMENTS

So much of the Camino experience is in the meeting of souls. This book would not have been possible without the many wonderful people I bonded with on the Camino Aragonese, the Camino del Norte, the Camino Primitivo and the Camino Frances. Special thanks go to my wife, Alyce and my good friend Tom, who walked parts of the Camino with me. Thanks also to Tim Obojski for the textual suggestions.

CHAPTER ONE — LOST

My left foot slipped dangerously close to the edge, making me lose balance and fall hard to the ground.

Thunder snapped like a whiplash cracking the air, the lightning striking the rock face just ahead, echoing into the valley below with a ricocheting crescendo.

It was cold and I was lost in the Pyrenees mountains along the border between France and Spain. It was late, dusk was approaching. An invisible cold hand seemed to grip at my throat.

Lying face down, I stared into what seemed like a deep dark hole below. It was fear and at the same time mesmerizing, tempting.

One slip, one step and I would be falling, falling. It seemed so easy. It would be one way of telling the world to get lost.

The exhaustion, the pain. At that point, I had found myself in a spiral of complete hopelessness. It could have been the way out. I moved closer to the edge. What if I hit a ledge on the way down, with death taking days and making me endure excruciating pain?

Before I could find the answer, thunder struck again with such force that I felt myself yanked from the ground, and hitting the rock wall behind me.

I felt my ears ringing as if being hit by a hard hand, my heart pounding against my chest, all muscles taut with fear and the sudden rush of adrenaline.

I looked around, bulging my fists, bracing for the next wave, until realizing that there was nothing.

I was completely alone.

After what seemed like an eternity I tried to get up, feeling again the sharp pain in my left knee, the blisters on my toes and the pain in my lower back.

Finally, shaking unsteadily on my feet with the far too heavy backpack weighing me down, I continued the climb.

I had to continue. Spending the night in the cold and the rain was no alternative. Many a hiker had gotten lost here before and frozen to death in the bone-chilling night temperatures.

The snapping thunder behind me was like a clarion call telling me to just keep on walking.

It was getting late. Darkness was setting in. Once again it had been my wandering thoughts, a lack of awareness that made me miss the last waymarker on what was in fact a clearly marked trial to Col du Somport in Spain.

Thoughts of the events just prior to my departure on the flight to Toulouse had once again sidetracked me.

It had been a spontaneous decision to go on a walk. I was unprepared for the physical and emotional challenges that come with those first days of loneliness.

"Is there anybody out there?"

A gust of wind, fanning the trees was the only answer.

What was that force that had pulled me from the crevice? My mind must be playing games – too much emotional stress over the past few months.

Yet, an inner voice seemed to urge me on: "Just keep walking."

Taking a rest was no alternative. The cold, wet mountain air was creeping through every pore of my body.

"Please, God, help me find a way to get out of here;" I pleaded. Waiting for death from exposure to the elements must be one of the worst ways to die.

Then in the distance the echo of ringing cowbells. The all too familiar sound that was so comforting. It was like the chime of a "welcome home" ceremony, like a wake-up call and the first sign of civilization.

A clearing. The smell of fresh dew and grass. A cow lazily picked up its head while the other animals in the herd took no notice. A path? Finally, Lights in the distance. All I needed was to follow the trail downhill.

It is amazing what power the human body can tap

from unknown resources. I increased my pace.

"Careful, Jake!" At this point I could not risk a fall or an injury, forcing me to stay out in the cold.

I had forgotten the blisters and the pain. It took me another two hours before I hit the tarred road that led me straight into the village and the only inn in town. The landlady, in a purple dressing gown, looked sheepishly from her desk and put aside the glossy magazine she was reading.

"People are not careful in areas they don't know," she said.

"Happens every summer and sometimes even in winter. Costs a taxpayer lots of money to go out and find them in the mountain with a rescue team."

I was not in any mood to argue.

CHAPTER TWO — CHUCK

A bear followed me through the forest, cornering me on a narrow ledge, bearing its teeth and lunging at me with a massive paw.

Then it was on top of me, pinning me to the ground. Somehow, I managed to free myself but was falling down that ledge with frightening speed, then was wedged between two rocks, unable to move.

I woke from that nightmare, my body bathed in sweat, my heart pounding as if I had run a marathon, my blistered feet hurting.

It was close to 7 a.m. I could have done with more sleep. I attended to a blister on my right toe opening it with a scissor so that the fluid could ooze out, and using a special hiker's plaster to close the wound.

The landlady was a lot more cheerful in the morning, serving me a coffee and a fresh croissant. It was France and the French are not into having a sumptuous breakfast. I left Bedous at 7.30, limping along at a slow pace as best I could.

Outside a camping site I found a trash bin and started shedding some of the clutter in my backpack. It was unnecessary eating utensils, a heavy ground sheet, several items of clothing, an extra pair of shoes, books, pots.

Shedding that weight made walking with my injured feet a lot easier. I had not heeded Claire's advice that "every kilogram in your backpack will start feeling like 10 kilograms." I had to learn the hard way, stubborn as I was.

My mind was wandering into a dark pit of nothingness. I had started my pilgrimage in Lourdes and been on the path for a week. I was two days behind schedule, having lost much time losing my way and having to go slow with a low-quality backpack loaded with clutter.

I would at most reach Urdos, still a stretch from the French-Spanish border at Somport.

I had been working for my newspaper for 20 years and now it was no more - apart from an online edition with our once large and experienced editorial team laid off.

For many years I had enjoyed my work as a correspondent, reporting on many of the world's political hotspots. Job cuts in the media industry, had reduced journalism to regurgitating information.

Bound to a desk was a far cry from experiencing world events firsthand. Like my job, the relationship I had been in had become sour.

"If you decide to leave me alone here to go to Spain, then you will come back to an empty apartment with the divorce papers in the mail," my wife warned me.

I decided to go anyway. Nothing could stop the urge to walk the Camino.

"We will see each other when we see each other," I said as I took my backpack and walked out the door.

It was the end of a seven-year marriage, yet I felt no urge, nor had the energy, to defend, justify and explain.

There had been too much of it. "Well, you did this ... You did that."

" I'm not happy in our relationship because ..."

After the communication breakdown came long moments of silence, the realization dawning.

We had nothing more in common, nothing more to talk about. The witty, easy going tolerance of each other during romance was gone.

There is a sadness about what once was, which lasts for a while until the tension underlying the disappointment, loss of love and compassion is overwhelmed by angry outbursts and irritability.

Couples fall in love and then fall out of it. I had been in three relationships that ended in the seventh year and was disappointed and angry at myself for having failed.

It was a common pattern to stay in jobs and relationships that had long outlived their usefulness.

Lessons that had to be learned had long been learned, and for too long I had just been going through the motions like a sad song in replay mode.

The result was growing irritability, bouts of sickness, lack of sleep, fatigue and a general loss of meaning and purpose.

This time, I said to myself, I would not again stumble into a new relationship. I needed time for reflection and a reset button for what I wanted for the rest of my remaining lifetime.

I was following an inner calling, an answer to so many of life's big questions, and I was not finding that answer by staying in a comfort zone.

If I continued staying in that groove, that supposed comfort zone, fate would strike with a serious illness or death – that much my higher self was telling me.

A part of me was deeply aware that each one of us lives for a purpose, has unique talents and abilities. I was unhappy because I had lost direction and purpose.

The Camino de Santiago has been one of the most important Christian pilgrimage routes for over 1,000 years. It is a network of paths leading from every major European city to Santiago de Compostela.

Several hundred thousand people walk the route each year. And a good friend, Claire, who had walked it the previous year, mentioned it to me the first time.

"Just try it, Jake. For me it was life-changing, and maybe you will find the answers you are looking for on the Camino," she said.

"Just be open to the mystery of the path," she said, giving me a guide book to read.

Perhaps it was more her messianic enthusiasm that convinced me and not the idea, as the guide book explained, of going on a modern-day "pilgrimage."

Also, known as the St. James Way, the Camino was one of the most important Christian pilgrimage routes in the Middle Ages. According to legend, the remains of James, one of the first disciples of Jesus, were buried on a hilltop in Santiago, after his martyrdom at the hands of Herod Agrippa.

A larger number of pilgrims from beyond the Pyrenees began walking to the shrine of St. James around the 11th century. They were on the road for months, and many died from disease, physical exhaustion or other ailments.

The Camino has survived to this day. Despite centuries when the number of pilgrims diminished to a trickle because of political turmoil and wars.

For me it was an opportunity to get away on a search for meaning at a time when my life was falling apart. Claire had warned me:

"I need to tell you this, Jake.

"Remain humble on the path, or the path will humble you."

And, the path was certainly teaching me humility in more ways than I had imagined.

I had hardly left Lourdes when I got lost the first time in drenching rain.

The path was well marked, but if your mind wanders,

and a dozen monkeys dance in your head, the red-blue way markers on trees and stones are easily overlooked.

I had followed Claire's advice by starting my pilgrimage along the Arles route in Lourdes. I was neither a Catholic nor a devout Christian, my journalistic cynicism having replaced any religious notions.

It seemed logical to choose an easier route where I could spend the first days getting warmed up on short 12 – to 15 kilometer stages, rather than starting the Camino Frances at St. Jean Pied de Port, a bustling French town in the foothills of the Pyrenees.

"St. Jean is where most people start the Camino Frances. It is beautiful but a tough one if you go there unprepared, like you are," Claire had warned me.

From St Jean, it was a steep climb, winding to an altitude of 1,430 meters before descending into Roncesvalles for a good 27 kilometers. Every year hikers get lost in bad weather and freak storms have claimed many a pilgrim's life.

After I left the train station at Lourdes, it started raining. I followed the signs to the famous grotto and stopped at a tavern to put on my rain jacket.

"This my property. You want to eat or drink, you stay, otherwise go!" the irate tavern owner said, motioning at me as if I were a vagrant.

I felt anger rise in me but was too tired to start a fight. I walked past rows and rows of shops selling religious mementos when I heard a voice behind me. "Peregrino! Peregrino!"

A kind lady showed me the way to the pilgrim's hostel, a short walk up a hill. I was happy to have found a place to stay.

The 14-year old peasant girl Bernadette Soubirous had the first of 18 apparitions on February 11, 1858. Her younger sister, Toinette, and their friend Jeanne Abadie were out looking for firewood near the grotto of Massabielle in Lourdes.

After taking off her shoes to walk through a nearby stream, Bernadette suddenly feels a gust of wind. Looking up at the grotto, she sees, in the upper corner of the rock wall, a beautiful lady, wearing a white dress with a blue belt and a yellow rose on each foot.

Bernadette falls to the ground and does not move. But then the lady signals to Bernadette with her finger to come closer. Bernadette grabs her rosary and tries to make the sign of the cross. But she is unable to do this until the lady, who is also carrying a rosary with a large, shining crucifix has made the sign of the cross.

The lady lets the beads slide through her fingers without moving her lips. The vision lasts for a good 15 minutes. The other girls see nothing.

By July 16th of 1858 Bernadette experiences a total of 18 apparitions. She confides to the girl in a gentle voice that she is the lady clothed in the sun, the completely pure one.

Word spreads and crowds of people come to Lourdes for the apparitions, which are only seen by Bernadette.

The local police and clergymen interrogate her. She is

even ordered to stay away from the grotto.

The descriptions of the beautiful lady are vivid but some of the officials believe the girl is imagining things, unstable and mentally ill.

Then a newly ordained priest from a town close to Massabielle takes his time to study Bernadette intently. His verdict: "What perfect peace! What perfect serenity! What a perfect saintliness! It's impossible for a child to make this up; so pure, so beautifully lovely.

"I felt as though I was standing on heaven's threshold."

Bernadette is told by the lady that she wants many people to come to that place, and to command the priests to build a chapel there.

Today it is one of the world's most visited shrines, drawing some 5 million people to the small French town every year. Miraculous cures have been documented in Lourdes. Others have come, hoping and praying for a miracle cure or the healing of a loved one, only to fall into despair or loss of faith when the prayer is not answered.

I observe the procession at the shrine from a distance that evening. People in wheelchairs. People being carried on stretchers. People walking and holding candles with the light flickering in their faces, telling me that the shrine was a place of reflection of looking deeply inward at both the wounds and the light within and the restoration of the spirit.

In the niche of the grotto where the lady appeared to

Bernadette stands a statue of the Virgin Mary, illuminated against the rock, like a beacon of light coming from a dark chasm in the depths of the earth.

On that first day of my pilgrimage I felt the fear and loneliness. The power of the place was overwhelming. I was not ready. It would take me some time to go beyond scratching the surface of my superficial observations.

The next day saw me running, running from that inexplicable energy that could not be explained with a rational mind, the hurt and the pain within me clasping at my throat like a hand of iron.

The drenching rain and the first blisters forced me to slow my pace to a slouching, muddy slog and feeling very sorry for myself.

I got as far as Betharram. It was a 17-kilometer (10.5 mile) walk from Lourdes which would have taken a normal hiker 3.5 hours but took me over seven. It was my first day of walking and I needed a full day to recover.

I was not in a good physical shape, to put it mildly. Claire had advised me to do some training and at least go for longer walks before commencing on the Camino with a back pack.

It was my first lesson in humility and there were more to come. I couldn't imagine how the pilgrims of the Middle Ages managed to walk an average of 3,000 kilometers from the doorsteps of their homes to Santiago and back.

There was no more running away. My aching body

was forcing me to slow down, and in that way forcing me to feel each step and every emotion as I trudged along.

I was forced to look around me, to smell the herbs along the path, to see the butterflies flutter around me, hear the birds in the trees and bear with the hours of silence and loneliness that were becoming unbearable. I was longing just to speak to someone.

Enduring my own presence, thoughts and emotions without the easily accessible distractions of daily life was a bigger challenge than I had ever imagined possible. I was forced to glare into the chasm of the self.

I felt the need to meet, talk to people in my own language about anything just to escape the cauldron of pent-up emotions and feelings that had been locked away somewhere deep in my sub conscious and seemed to get bigger with every step of every hour every day.

I met a French couple whose English was just as bad as my French. "She is crazy," he would say at regular intervals, to which she would respond:

"No, he is crazy." I gathered that they had met on the path and were both on vacation without their spouses, supporting each other on the walk in some strange, teasing way. He was a government official from Paris and she a red-haired hairdresser from Nantes. After a while our efforts to find a level of communication must have been too frustrating. I reduced my pace while they increased their paces and disappeared over the next hill.

A Dutch cyclist had a need for a conversation, and slowed down next to me. He was a former banker who found himself in early retirement at the age of 58 after "restructuring measures."

"Join the club," I told him, and we shared our disappointment about former employers who felt no remorse at laying off employees who had been loyal to their company for decades.

"My wife sent me on the Camino. She told me to go because I was getting on her nerves sitting on the sofa all day. So here I am, Jan, who has come all the way from Amsterdam. You might feel it in your legs but I'm feeling it in my butt, every day when I stop.

Before wishing me a "buen camino, maybe I'll see you." He suggested kindly that I should get a much smaller backpack. I thought that I had rid myself from all the unnecessary clutter after leaving Bedous.

But the straps on my back pack were coming loose and chafing the skin off my shoulder.

I was still carrying too much. It was symbolic of all the emotional baggage I carried with me at the start of my journey.

My feet, my knees, my back were hurting again. I was once more at an emotional low and I decided then and to just walk to my next destination in Sarrance and catch the bus that would take me back to Toulouse and a flight home to Ireland.

What had driven me to think that I could walk several hundred kilometers to Santiago? I was in no physical shape to do so. I hated myself. I hated the Camino. I ridiculed all the pilgrims. This was ridiculous. No more nights in mundane hostels. This was it.

The pilgrim hostel in Sarrance is situated in the old monastery on the southern edge of the village, which I reached until late that afternoon, slouching, hurting and in a bad mood.

Adding to my foul temper was a sign outside the only tavern in town saying it was closed. I couldn't find the bus stop where I could head back in the direction I had come. Back home that was for me. I walked in circles until I came back to the waymark that showed me the route to the albergue or pilgrim hostel.

Our mood and emotional state depends on what we see around us. It took me a while to see the beauty of the village I was in.

According to legend, a chapel was built in Sarrance during the Middle Ages after an apparition of the Virgin Mary.

The 12th century church was destroyed during wars of religion and was rebuilt in the 17th century. One of the lateral chapels holds an altarpiece from the 18th century that narrates how an image of the Virgin was found by a beautiful bull.

The bull appeared in town each day but nobody could catch it, so the townsfolk decided to follow it into the forest to a mysterious spring where it bowed and prayed to the image of Mary.

The image was then moved to a cathedral in Oloron, but Mary always returned to her original spot, where she wanted to be worshipped.

In the church, the head of a black virgin - the earliest representation of the Virgin of Sarrance is the only piece that survived the destruction of the church in 1569.

Reconstruction began in 1605 and continued for 70 years in a Baroque style the church placing emphasis on penitence, preaching and meditation. It was in the courtyard of the adjacent monastery that I noticed a couple of pilgrims enjoying the cool and meditative atmosphere.

After attending to the daily procedure of doing my wash, having a shower and treating my blistered feet, I went into the courtyard of the monastery with the firm intention of announcing to the pilgrims there that this was the end of my Camino. I had had enough. They could all go and finish their walk. But this Camino thing was nothing for me.

I noticed a guy with an American drawl talking to some pilgrims. He had a carefully trimmed goatee, and this shiny, long black hair streaked with gray kept in place with a colorful headband. He was wearing a long jacket that reached almost to his ankles.

A lost Californian hippie from the 1970s, was my first thought. He exuded a warmth that attracted people all around him and forced me to listen in on the conversation.

"The Mother shows herself as the nurturer, protector and life-giving force. It was actually long before the arrival of Christianity that the Basques worshipped the female Goddess, who lived in the caves, along the streams and in the mountains. Interestingly, they called her Mari, with all the humans and spirits under her order.

"The legend of Sarrance is typical of many of the stories you will find along the Camino. Mary reveals herself in caves, grottos and in natural surroundings, pulling us mortal beings back to nature so that we can reconnect with our souls and find our true nature in the bigger picture of things."

Somehow, I could relate to that.

"In becoming civilized and living in big cities we seem to have lost something," I said.

Despite my hardships and frustration that day, I had to admit that I had also enjoyed some parts of my walk. I was beginning to feel the nature. I had noticed the sunlight shining through the tunnel of trees onto the waters of the Aspe River.

Hearing the rushing of the waters nearby had a greatly calming and soothing effect, and I took the time to wash my blistered feet in the cold water.

My energy started returning and we were all looking forward to the warm meal being prepared for us.

Instead of announcing my plans to end the Camino, I shared my impressions of Lourdes.

"I felt the power of the place but I was kind of turned off by the commercialization of religion you find there," I said.

"Everywhere you go you find these crosses and little statues of Mary, probably all mass-produced in China."

The American, who introduced himself as Chuck, looked at me, sensing my sarcasm.

"You could see it that way, dude. But think of these trinkets bringing the energy of Lourdes to the tens of thousands of people in the cancer clinics, old age homes and sick beds."

He had a point, and I had the habit of seeing the negative rather than the positive. It was a conscious choice on what we wanted to see, and it was a choice "on which side of the fence you fall on."

Chuck looked at me intently, as if sensing my thoughts:

"Just keep on walking, dude. You are capable of more than you think."

The words triggered something in me. I had boxed myself into my own thought chamber and it needed someone like Chuck to pull me from my despair.

Instead of focusing on the beautiful walk along the Aspe River that day, I had decided to fall into negative desperation when my body started hurting at the end of my day's hike.

I would give it another day, I said to myself.

"You, are capable of more than you think," I whispered to myself.

There were about 10 of us at the dinner table that evening. An old priest greeted each one and said grace for about five minutes. I couldn't understand the words. But a young French man with a mane of curly black hair rolled his eyes and shook his head.

He certainly wanted none of this prayer business and was only waiting to dig into the spaghetti bolognese and the homemade bread.

We got involved in an animated discussion. Contrary to my first impression, the old priest was a humorous guy, chuckling happily as he listened to the stories told by the pilgrims and kindly offering each one of us more wine as the evening wore on.

He must have heard many similar stories over the years, but I just had to admire his patience and the genuine interest.

CHAPTER THREE — FAMILY ISSUES

We were all on a journey and felt a connection to each other like of friends who have known each other for years.

So, I was disappointed at not having had the opportunity of saying goodbye to the new friends I had made the previous evening.

I had overslept, once again, and was one of the last ones to leave that morning.

There was Pierre, a jovial French businessman from Paris, who spoke excellent English and helped prepare the salad and the spaghetti bolognese spiced with fresh herbs.

And there was a young German couple, Anja and Bernd, who were taking time off from their studies to do the Camino.

"I never thought it would be so hard. We started in Oloron and my knee hurts. I thought I was fit," Anja complained.

We compared notes on our physical and emotional ailments and the reasons why we were walking the Camino.

"The first part of the Camino is like a crucifixion," Pierre joined in.

"In a way, you're right," Chuck said "Yeah, you wanna get all the muck to the surface and walk it off." He was the only experienced pilgrim among us, having walked the Camino several times.

Chuck, it turned out, was of Irish, American Indian and Spanish ancestry. He had left his Californian home to settle in a village about 150 kilometers from Santiago some five years ago, "a calling," he confided with a positive intensity that frightened me.

Was he one of those born-again Christians out to impose religion on everyone that crossed his path? But he did not touch the issue again.

All of us had chosen the Aragon route for different reasons, but mainly to avoid the crowds on the "Camino Highway" the main path from Saint-Jean-Pied-de-Port.

From the Aragon route, Chuck was going on to the Camino del Norte, the coastal route from Bilbao, while the others were planning to continue on the Camino Frances at Puenta la Reina. Pierre was planning to end his Camino in Burgos.

The Aragon route, we learned from Chuck, was the true Camino Frances. During the Middle Ages, most of the pilgrims from Germany, Scandinavia and Poland would meet at the monastery in Einsiedeln, near Geneva, for the last mass before taking the Arles route in France that would eventually take them over the Pyrenees at Somport through the Spanish kingdom of Aragon.

Before leaving Urdos, I had a coffee and croissant in a café, where I met a fellow pilgrim, Greta from Sweden. She was in her late 40s with blonde hair tied in a ponytail. The mixture of sadness, perhaps even anger, in her blue-green eyes, indicated she was carrying much old baggage with her.

At first I thought she was one of those pilgrims who wanted to be alone, but she seemed relieved to strike up a conversation with me and like most Swedes, spoke excellent English.

We walked out of Urdos together, passing a massive crucifix at the side of the road. All the pain and suffering of Jesus were emphasized in the stone-carved facial features with the wind, rain and sun leaving their marks on the material.

"This is one of my issues with Christianity … always they want us to see the suffering, the pain. It's like bearing a cross on your back all your life. Where is the joy in all this?" she said.

"It's like we always want to kill something as a sacrifice so that we feel good inside, or to appease an angry God."

"So why are you walking the Camino?" I asked out of curiosity, trying to get behind the sadness in her eyes. "You will be confronted by the crucifix in almost every village we go through."

"I don't really know," she said, already gasping for air from the short walk out of the village.

"Maybe I want to sacrifice something. I've only been walking a few days and it's been like a crucifixion. But I don't want to hold you up. You go ahead. Maybe we'll see each other at Somport."

Something told me that Greta was not doing well. I decided to walk on but to keep her within eyesight, just in case. She seemed overly frail, walking a little unsteadily and off balance, and carrying a backpack too big and heavy for her small body.

The path took us along a busy road with heavy-duty trucks whooshing past too close for my liking.

That did not detract from the beauty around us. The mountaintops on the left were still capped with snow. Birds of prey circled against the backdrop of a deep blue sky.

We passed the Fort du Portalet, built into the cliff face to the left of the road and overlooking the Aspe. Built by order of Louis Philippe I in the mid-19th century, the massive fortress once guarded access to the Somport Pass along the border with Spain. I noticed Greta stop to take some pictures and a long swig from her water bottle.

At last the Path took a turn to the left into a forest, winding its way up the steep mountain to the Somport (1,632 meters or 5,354 feet).

I waited until I saw Greta coming around the corner. We stopped at a stream further up the mountain, refilled our water bottles and shared a lunch of goat cheese, olives and a baguette. Greta even produced half a bottle of red wine from her backpack.

"Voilà, I did not carry this all the way for nothing," she said pouring the wine into two plastic cups.

"Skål – cheers, and thanks for waiting. I could have missed that turn up the hill, and I hate walking on a busy road."

We walked through a herd of cows with bells hanging from their necks, the ringing echoing from afar. It was a slow, steady climb along the well-marked path.

White butterflies flew around like petals blowing in the wind. The path took us through shady forest and then along treeless green meadows. We felt the cold alpine air brush our faces as we left the forest cover and the rocky, mountain peaks ahead.

After a good three hours, we finally reached Somport. There we saw familiar faces - Chuck and the German couple having a beer.

Together we enjoyed the spectacular view with a beer and a late afternoon lunch.

Typical for this mountain country, the weather changed rapidly within the next half hour.

Dark storm clouds were gathering in the distance. We debated whether to stay overnight at Somport or move on to Canfranc-Estacion, which was another three-hour walk away and a steep downhill.

The break had given us a burst of energy. Greta found that Somport had "too little Camino atmosphere" with all the day tourists around.

Chuck walked on ahead with the rest of us following, passing the ruins of the Santa Cristina Hospital, where he gave us a brief rundown of its history. Founded in the 12th century, it was one of the most important hospitals in the Christian world, built on a spot where many a tired, ill and exhausted pilgrim needed care.

On our right, we passed an unsightly gray hotel complex that was part of a major ski resort in the winter months. Construction of a new highway had destroyed an old part of the route that once passed along beautiful rock pools.

Ominous thunder in the distance made us increase our pace, and then we heard a thud, followed by a low moan of pain. It was Greta.

She was lying facedown, unable to get up with her backpack pinning her to the ground, her sunglasses lying in pieces.

We unstrapped her backpack and tried to help her up. Her face was covered in dust and a sleeve was torn with blood oozing from her arm. Skin was chafed off her right shinbone and knee.

" No! It's hurting. I have to sit down."

The initial shock over, Greta burst into tears." I should have listened to my family. They warned me not to go. I can't walk any more..."

"You don't seem to have broken any bones. Lots of bruises and scrapes that need some attention, though," Chuck, comforted her.

We helped her to a nearby stream, where we cleaned and bandaged her knee and arm. We distributed the contents of her backpack amongst us to reduce the weight and took turns half carrying, half pulling her to Canfranc-Estacion, which we reached as darkness set-in. Just after entering the cozy albergue, the heavens opened to a massive downpour.

We found a comfortable bed for Greta. The hospitalera, a charming Spanish woman, brought her a warm soup. Someone offered to call a doctor to check her over, but Chuck intervened, saying that would not be necessary.

During the course of the evening, Greta opened up to us.

"They told me I needed chemo after I had a tumor removed from my breast. I refused and they told me I would die if I didn't do the chemo.

"Hearing the word "cancer" is like a death sentence. I know I won't die but there is still that fear that comes when I wake up at night. I've always wanted to do the Camino. I really don't want to stop here and go home."

"So, tell me Greta, why then did you fall today?" Chuck asked.

Tears ran down Greta's cheeks. Chuck gently took her hand." Are you open to having a cleansing ritual?" Greta nodded.

"I'll do some smudging with some sage. It's good to get the air around you cleared."

Chuck placed a bunch of sage in an earthen pot and lit

27

it with a match, allowing it to burn a little. Once there was enough smoke, he took a feather and waved the smoke around Greta, all the time humming and saying prayers or mantras, which could have been American Indian or some other native language. Chuck's entire composure and posture changed.

He walked slowly around the room, continuing to say his prayers, eyes closed in deep concentration. This was a different man. It was as if he had flipped a switch, slipped into the robe of an ancient Indian shaman and in the cloud of smoke his facial features changed. Was I imagining things or was he wearing a headdress of feathers and a bearskin cloak. The half-darkness in the poorly lit room must have been playing tricks with my imagination.

Loud thunder could be heard outside. Heavy raindrops, rattled the windows like demons trying to get in? The atmosphere in the room changed. Chuck's humming voice turned deeper and more incessant, then became calm and reversed to a low, hardly audible hum.

Greta opened her eyes." Thank you. I feel much better."

"You need to rest for a day. You have your answer."

"Yes, I do ... and many more other questions."

I had an uncomfortable night, waking from the incessant rain outside, thinking. Cancer was a demon that had stalked me from an early age. Greta's moan of pain was the same that I had known from my own mother.

The disease is brutal in the way it seizes people when needed most and in the midst of life. All those years I had suppressed the pain of having lost her when I was in my teens, leaving me surrounded by helpless siblings and a father, who dealt with his grief by falling into silent depression.

There were only a few months between the diagnosis and her death. I remember the many friends and relatives, with their own advice on how to deal with the illness.

A flicker of hope came after the first chemo treatment, then the cancer returned, striking with brutal inevitability and speed. Weeks of hope and prayer in the intensive unit. Maybe a miracle? It was not to be. The hospital room felt strangely empty when the last breath left her body. A doctor came by with a stethoscope, his head drooped. It was over.

The priest did his duty, telling us about God calling the best of souls to heaven. But I was angry. I lost my faith. What kind of God allowed this to happen? Did we not all pray for healing? Was my mother not a devout Christian who wanted to live to see her grandchildren grow up. This was a cruel God and I wanted no part of him. Prayers didn't work. This was all a myth and a big lie designed to control and manipulate.

I sensed the same anger in Greta. Once again, here was a woman, who wanted to live and enjoy life. Cancer appeared to strike at random, irrespective of whether that person was a devout believer, agnostic, atheist or political activist.

Greta looked surprisingly good the next morning. "Looks like I've been beaten by a bad man. I am blue all over," she said. Anja, whose knee was still hurting, decided to stay with her at the hostel. They would take a bus and meet us in Jaca, a good 4.5- hour walk.

Chuck gave us a brief rundown of the impressive Canfranc Estacion railway station on our left. It was opened in 1928 with great pomp and ceremony as a shining jewel of Art Nouveau elegance, linking the French city of Pau with the Spanish city of Zaragossa.

It was a massive engineering feat to build the more than 80 bridges through the Pyrenees mountains. But the line was never profitable and was hit by the Great Depression in the 1930s, a major fire and the Spanish Civil War in 1936. It had a brief run of glory in 1965, when it served as a set for the famous film Dr. Zhivago, and was finally shut down in the early 1970s after a train accident.

In the morning fog the gray-domed building with the rusty railway lines in front of it looked like a monument from another world, a palace haunted by the ghosts of the rich and famous from a bygone age.

I didn't have much energy to reflect on the story of supposed Nazi gold. There were tales from the locals, describing border officials offloading massive amounts of gold bars and art treasures at Canfranc during World War II.

I was having to deal with the ghosts of my own past, memories of several broken relationships and the cynicism that grew with every year I got older. I had many issues to walk off and rapidly increased my pace to leave Chuck and Bernd some distance behind.

They caught up with me at the Canfranc bridge, an ancient, curved structure built by a man called Ramón de Argelas in 1599 on the ruins of an even older bridge washed away by floodwaters of the Aragon river.

I apologized for my silent brooding. "It's been like this for some days. I have old issues to deal with. And then this cancer thing comes up."

"It's normal during the first days of walking. Congratulations. You are dealing with the old ghosts that lurk in your sub consciousness. This is where the healing work starts on the Camino," Chuck said, giving me a gentle pat on the back.

"So, the other pilgrims were right. The first part of the Camino is like going through a crucifixion. We were both standing at that crucifix outside Urdos, feeling disturbed by the image."

"Yeah, there are a lot of misunderstandings about Christianity. It took me a while to figure it out. Terrible wars have been fought and millions of people killed over the issue of the true believer. There has been so much suffering because of religion. That's not what it's about. Religion is about an organized belief system; spirituality is an authentic belief that comes from within. It's a discovery, a journey that each one of us has to take individually. The messages that we hear out there can merely serve as guidance for that discovery. God speaks to you on a personal, one-to-one level.

"This must be one of the reasons, so many people are

now walking the Camino," I said. "I've had a problem with this old-man God figure for a long time."

Bernd meanwhile joined us, listening closely. "I've never had that problem. I was raised Catholic in a small Bavarian town. It is just part of the culture I grew up in."

I related my thoughts of that morning. "So, if God is almighty, why doesn't he intervene?"

"Sorry if I'm blunt, dude, but you are skimming the surface, like most people when you ask the question that way. Suffering is part of our being in this world. We have this picture of wanting to strive for a paradise that will never be reality. Yeah, we have come a long way from the dark Middle Ages..."

"And there are many parts of the world today in worse shape than the Middle Ages," I chipped in.

"There is real evil in this world," Chuck added "We are forgetting that Satan is alive and well and fighting the good that is from God in many cloaks and guises. The worst ruse is that he is trying to make us believe that he doesn't exist.

"It's a choice we make every day. Do you choose to take the path of light or do you go the dark route? Do you confront your ego, your dark emotions and fears, or do you trust, in love and compassion? It's from this duality that we grow, that we evolve and serve the bigger whole.

"Jesus made the ultimate sacrifice in giving his life to make us understand that it's all about coming from the heart, about love and compassion not only for our fellow man but primarily about accepting and loving ourselves. It's as simple as that. Forget all the bullshit you hear otherwise."

Chuck was talking as we walked. He picked up a flat stone and placed it into my hand. "Put it on the pile of stones you'll find on the road markings with the scallop shell. Start with your parents and then pick a stone for each family line, going through the generations."

I learned that it was a tradition of medieval pilgrims. The wealthy would send at least one family member to Santiago to cleanse the family of sins. The not-so-wealthy collected money from the other family members to enable one of them to go.

"In our Indian culture, we show great respect for our ancestors. If we lose the connection to where we come from, we lose our way. It's something all the ancient cultures have, by the way. But we modern people think we know it all. We need to reconcile and make peace with our parents, grandparents and family members to be able to move on."

Bernd came forward, offering an apple. "I need to get some stones too.

"It's not been good with Anja and myself the past two days. The problem with her knee started the day after she told me how hurt she was by her parents getting a divorce when she was a little girl. That turned up issues between her and me."

We continued our discussion for a while on the disconnect we felt was common in most families today. Chuck's view was that much of it came with the loss of ritual, eating meals together, having quality family time just spending more time talking to each other. Bernd argued that it was the excessive consumption of electronic media that stifled most communication.

The path took us along some beautiful stretches of road along the Aragon river. Behind us where the majestic Pyrenees as we gradually moved into flat country, stopping at a café to have coffee con leche and a bocadillo sandwich.

By late afternoon the temperature was well above 30 degrees Celsius (86 degrees Fahrenheit). A more than 20-kilometre walk was about as much I could manage at that point of my pilgrimage.

In the heat, the distances felt twice as long and a back-pack weighed heavily on the shoulders. I had placed many a stone on the scallop-shell road markings for family members, past relationships, broken friendships and deceased loved ones.

Each one of us had walked alone for the past two hours. Being alone was part of the Camino process, and I was beginning to cherish these moments of loneliness and reflection, digging into my own shadow self and not liking what I saw.

I was a "judgmental, self-indulgent, arrogant and cynical prick," to use the words of my ex-wife.

In the distance, I could see the town of Jaca in the valley below, with the spire of the Cathedral of St. Peter the Apostle in the center. It looked like a promising change from the many small villages we had passed through during the past few days.

After crossing a wooden bridge, I noticed Chuck waving me over. I waited for Bernd to catchup and we followed Chuck along an unmarked side-track. The rushing sound of waters came closer and the dense undergrowth opened up to a wonderful rock pool below us, fed by several streams of water from a cliff face above.

We needed no prompting to undress and take a swim in the turquoise-colored pool, the icy water making me catch my breath, the powerful stream massaging my aching shoulders and legs. It was just what we needed to replenish our energy for the final swing to Jaca.

I had mulled over the issue of pain and suffering. Were they predestined? Some people have a harsh life and others apparently an easy cruise. What about the nasties who seemed to be rewarded for their nastiness? It didn't make sense.

"Most suffering is emotional and in the mind. We need to distinguish between difficulties and problems. Most of the time we are dealing with difficulties and not problems, dude. Having a terminal illness is a problem, but I would say that not finding a place to sleep tonight, dude, that would be a minor difficulty in comparison.

"A difficulty starts becoming a problem when we cling to it and can't let go the things we have no influence over. There is a saying in Christianity that you should carry your cross through life. I would add that you should not let that cross become a burden, but to let that cross carry you.

"Pain and suffering comes from attachment. The

Buddhists call it the condition of samsara, the endless cycle of birth and death and wandering through a life with no purpose or direction, experiencing a bit of happiness here and a bit of sadness there, yet not really living.

"It's not that God wants us to suffer, dude. He wants us to live a happy, joyful life where we make our individual contribution to the happiness of fellow beings. But we are free beings."

"Who often make the wrong choices," I related, thinking of the many unhappy relationships I had more or less stumbled into.

"And you will make the same mistake and suffer the same consequences and pain of your action until you get it. You alone are responsible. Nobody is to blame - if you find yourself in a predicament."

I protested: "But freak accidents happen. Innocent people get bombed and shot by evildoers just because they are in the wrong place at the wrong time."

The images all came back at that moment. My assignment on the Iran-Iraqi border. Men, women and children fleeing the bombings by dictator Saddam Hussein. Dusty paths weaving along the rugged mountains where bloodied feet of the thousands of Kurdish refugees had crossed.

In a tented refugee village, a Red Cross doctor was desperately trying to save the life of a little girl, her body scorched horribly by a firebomb. There was no crying, no moaning, her body just shivering with pain.

I had seen them in Iraq, in Rwanda and in South Africa's township wars: children so tormented and traumatized that they could no longer cry or openly show emotion.

Evil in whatever form randomly destroys and wreaks havoc on innocent lives. The trauma remains etched in the mind for decades, for generations.

"Nothing happens without a reason. As I said this morning, dude. Satan is alive and well and he often lurks in the shadow where there is most light.

"But evil also tends to overreach itself and self-destruct. Look at Adolf Hitler, Saddam Hussein, Moamer Gaddafi. What you sow, you will reap. Karma, the consequences of actions, is slow, patient and inexorable.

"God comes into play when we forgive and stay in love and compassion. Think of Jesus: "Father, forgive them, for they don't know what they are doing.' It's a really powerful message. By going into the same hatred and darkness as the perpetrators, we aren't moving forward. We are perpetuating a conflict.

"I'm sounding preachy, I know," Chuck said. It's not that I know it all – I've been through rough times myself. I don't know whether I would have dug that deep spiritually if I hadn't lost my construction business in the recession of 2008 and my wife hadn't left with the kids.

"The point is, you want to avoid having to learn the lessons the hard way."

And I was really awaiting Chuck's take on that one.

But we had to move on. We still had some distance to cover that day.

CHAPTER FOUR — THE HOLY GRAIL

We reached the **Catedral de San Pedro Apóstol** in Jaca at dusk. It's an impressive building dating from the early 12th century, when Jaca became the capital of the Kingdom of Aragon.

Crowds of people were on the streets as life in Spain picked up in the early evening after the long afternoon siesta. A scent of incense was coming from behind the huge old oak doors of the Catedral.

We would have more time later in the evening to appreciate the full beauty of the building from inside.

Chuck, the experienced peregerino, again led the way to a narrow alleyway near the Catedral, where Greta and Anja were waiting for us in a private hostel. They were feeling guilty at having taken the bus, which took less than half an hour from Canfranc, while we had been on the road for more than six.

"I feel like I've been cheating," Anja said.

"I didn't really want to do the Camino this way," Greta added.

She began emptying her backpack. "All these things - I don't need to carry. I am so angry - angry at myself, angry at the world, angry at my ex-husband, angry at my children."

Chuck gave her a stern look: "Yeah, let out the anger, Greta. But why be so hard on yourself? You wanna take a break tomorrow? Rest and enjoy. Jaca is a beautiful town.

"You've just started emptying your backpack. The less clutter in your backpack - the more you go on trust."

"I don't need lectures from any man, least of all an American!" she retorted, throwing a shoe into the far corner of the room.

The end of a day walking on the Camino had a routine that started with a shower followed by the washing of socks, underwear and whatever gear was needed for the next day. On a warm night, the clothing was dry by the next day.

On a rainy or cold day, there was a scramble for every available radiator.

While going through our end-of-the-day peregrino routine, I noticed a lanky, bearded young man come up to me. He was hurting badly, feet bandaged, his face and arms sunburned. He told us his story. He had walked from Somport to Jaca on his first day – a 35-kilometer trek! (21.7 miles)

"My feet were hurting early on, but I just kept going and going. Then I got lost, found the path again, kept walking, walking. Luckily the Guardia Civil came by. They must have taken pity on me. They offered me a lift, took me right here to the hostel. No more walking for me."

The hostels posted notices in several languages, warning peregrinos not to walk in the hot afternoon sun so as to prevent death by dehydration.

"Remain humble or the path, or the path will humble you." Claire's words were present as ever.

Later, in the Catedral, I waited for the end of Mass. I could not follow the words of the Spanish priest but was impressed by the intensity, the play of light from the candles and the soft light from the ancient marble windows.

In the right corner was a statue of the Mother Mary with the light from the window behind her dazzling the floor. I did what I could do best when feelings overwhelmed me. I fled outside to catch some fresh air.

I found the others waiting for me. Chuck guessed my confusion.

"The Catedral San Pedro, is one of my favorites, probably goes back to a place of worship in pre-Christian times, like many of the places where the European cathedrals were built," Chuck commented.

"I don't like that painting with a guy's head chopped off on a plate. Why hang that up in a church? Yech!" Greta responded.

"St. John the Baptist. He was the prophet that baptized Jesus. Herod ordered him killed," Chuck said matter-of-factly.

"The Spaniards seem to have a liking for all this blood and gore," Greta remarked, about to pour some sugar into her cafe con leche.

"All these images you see of St. James slaughtering the Arabs, wars, fights, the Crusades – always blood."

At this point an elderly woman from across the table leaned over and grabbed Greta by the hand. There followed a flurry of words in Spanish that of course only Chuck could understand. The woman then said a silent prayer holding a rosary, turned and left, wishing us all "buen Camino!"

"What did she say?" Greta said, somewhat bewildered.

"That you should stay away from the sugar. If you don't, the cancer will kill you," Chuck said. "And that you should pray to the Mother. Ask for healing."

"You're not serious," she said. "How did she know I had cancer? She even knew my name!"

"Wait...where is she?" Greta got up from her stool, looking in the direction the woman had disappeared.

"You won't find her," Chuck said.

Greta turned pale. "What do you mean?"

"Nothing." He smiled.

"She probably lives around the corner here somewhere and enjoys talking to the peregrinos," I said.

Chuck's smug smile confused me.

As much as I enjoyed Jaca, I agreed to join Chuck the next day on a hike to the old monastery of San Juan de la Pena. It was an additional two-day hike up a steep mountain and off our main path which was a fairly straightforward walk to the next town.

I bought a new, smaller and lighter backpack at a trekking shop in Jaca, confident that I now had made the right choice. The less weight you carry, the easier your walk.

Prior to us getting into our beds that night, I noticed Greta and Chuck in deep conversation but it was none of my business. We all said goodnight and Greta gave Chuck and me a long, intense hug before wiping a tear from her cheek.

At that point, it was still unclear whether Greta could continue her walk. It filled me with sadness to know that we would perhaps never see her again.

We left the hostel at 6 a.m. to make the most of the cool morning air. I didn't sleep much that night as a group of revelers partied in the square outside until the wee hours.

It was a beautiful morning with a clear blue sky. The path soon took us up a steep mountain through a fir forest, from where we had a spectacular view of the snow-covered Pyrenees peaks in the distance and Jaca nestled in the valley below.

I was happy to follow Chuck, knowing that he would not get us lost in an area he had walked often.

We stopped later in the village of Ascara to fill our water bottles. I was still curious about the old woman we had met the night before.

"Do you really want to know?" Chuck asked.

"What do you think this is?" he asked, holding up his water bottle.

"A water bottle."

"What do you see around you?"

"A couple of old houses, a cat, and there is a woman hanging up laundry in her garden - seems to me the only person in this village."

"Yeah, but it's just one reality - that which is visible to the eye."

"Around us is an invisible reality that is like a matrix with different levels, layers and spirals. Creation is far more complex than we could ever imagine. We tend to look at things from a one-dimensional level. Imagine a three-dimensional, multi-dimensional reality, that is beyond the time and space we know.

"It is this invisible reality that we need to take seriously and make visible in the sense that it has great influence on the lives we live.

"Modern man thinks he knows it all. Science is merely the knowledge of what we define and know at a given moment in time."

Listening to Chuck, I was thinking this was all getting too esoteric for me. I wanted to know who that strange old woman was.

"So you think she was some kind of ghost or something? She looked pretty real to me."

"All I'm saying, dude, is that there are advanced souls, deceased many centuries ago, who walk between the worlds with a special mission, with a message for specific individuals. Some people might call them angels. They come in the guise of an old woman, a beggar, a priest, you name it, nothing spectacular. Some figure in angel wings would give you a darn big fright."

So if that were true, I asked, they could just as well be forces from the dark side.

"As I said, dude, Satan and his servants are alive and well. It is the other force, that at the first opportunity will seize what is pure and good, and you will also find it on the Camino. We need to be watchful - all the time - and I mean all the time."

"I think we should continue our walk," I said, sensing what was like a premonition.

Chuck was much faster as I had trouble keeping a good foothold on the steep, winding path littered with loose stones and rock. Fortunately, the cold water from the mountain stream was a welcome relief from the heat.

Then we finally reached our destination. Carved in a rocky outcrop was the ancient monastery of San Juan de la Pena. Dating back to the ninth century it became the spiritual and intellectual center of the Kingdom of Aragon. The monastery had enormous influence not only in the ancient kingdom, but throughout Europe in the early Middle Ages.

The monks lived disciplined lives, following a daily routine of contemplation, work and study. Silence was highly cherished. The monks took a vow of silence and were only allowed to speak if it was absolutely necessary or when it was a good thought or blessing. It was obviously an atmosphere conducive to highly-focused study and inner spiritual work.

The Holy Grail, the cup that was believed to have been used by Jesus during the Last Supper was used by Joseph of Arimathea to collect the blood of Jesus on the Cross. It was kept in the monastery for many centuries for protection from Muslim invaders.

"Call it coincidence or not, but the decline of the monastery began in the 14th century when the Aragonese King Martino V took the Holy Grail to his palace in Zaragoza.

When the monks asked for it back, he tricked them with a replica," Chuck related. "The original is kept today in the Cathedral of Valencia, and we know that the material it was made from stems from Roman times around the year 100."

"I don't really get it," I said as a large school class crowded around the replica positioned on the stone altar. "I've seen so many relics in the churches and cathedrals on the way here that I'm kind of wondering. There must have been a booming trade with fakes over the centuries. I have my doubts whether the real bones of St. James were ever buried in Santiago."

"There he goes again, the sceptic and cynical

intellectual dude.

"Some time ago I saw it the same way. And it's probably true that many of the relics are fakes. But in the Middle Ages they were real crowdpullers. An important relic became the focal point of pilgrimages, of faith and devotion. Every church building had to contain some relic before it could be consecrated. And come on, Dude. Don't we today value signatures, clothing or other utensils from famous people we admire."

"Look at the pulling power of Santiago. It started off with the bones of St. James becoming an object of worship hundreds of years ago, and this dynamic energy has lasted until today. And whether the Holy Grail was really the vessel from which Jesus drank wine with his disciples. Who knows? Who cares? It's really about the Holy Grail triggering the question: Where is the Holy Grail within you?"

"It's about the positive energy generated by the tens of thousands of people who visit Lourdes, Santiago or relics of a saint or martyr. That is what it's really about...It's this positive energy that nurtures the Holy Grail within."

For the monks at San Juan de la Pena, the loss of the Holy Grail must have been traumatic, setting the stage for gradual decay. After a fire destroyed much of the monastery in 1675, the Monasterio Nuevo, or new monastery was built further up the mountain.

There were several fires that destroyed much of the monastery complex in the 17th century. Decay came with infighting and power struggles. Grants and privileges from the king were reduced and at times completely stopped. Loss of focus and purpose set-in with vows being broken and poor leadership.

The mountain's majestic beauty was a powerful inspiration for contemplation and self-reflection. Leaving the old monastery and taking the path downhill, I discovered an open meadow and a spot for a rest under a shady tree, and fell asleep.

I woke to the sound of bird song. Butterflies were dancing over the field of blooming white flowers. Some distance away I heard the trickling spring. A gust of wind surged through the trees, rustling the leaves like some giant hidden hand, followed by total silence.

Then the veil lifted: I felt my heart beating like some distant echoing drum, and this moment enormous joy and happiness enveloped me. The white flowers with the dancing butterflies took on a particular hue of silver and gold in the late afternoon sun.

God is creation itself, the Creator of the universe. We are a product and part of this vast expanse of interconnectedness.

Our purpose is to become aware of our part in this great evolutionary cycle and that we are a ray from and part of the Creator, true to the biblical passage that we are made in the image of God.

God is pure spirit and if God is immortal as pure spirit, then we, too, are immortal as spirit beings, death being a mere passage of that giant wheel of evolution.

CHAPTER FIVE — HEAD MIND, HEART MIND

"Your first thought of the day when waking very often determines your day. Have a bad dream and a bad thought and you will likely be grumpy all day. Have a good thought or say a good prayer and you most likely will have a good day.

"It's a matter of conscious choice at every moment in time," Chuck said, inviting me to his meditation after noticing my morning grumpiness.

It was a simple meditation concentrating on counting the in and exhalating breaths, relaxing the body and letting all other thoughts go by, a practice of staying in the here and now.

I had experienced the first lifting of the veil the day before, a ray of light that was beginning to penetrate the shadow of consciousness, stirring a deep yearning for entry into a new reality. At the same time, it was unknown and confusing territory.

"That yearning is a good sign," Chuck told me as we began our walk downhill to Santa Cilia. "It's like that at the beginning, and you won't want to go back to a life behind the veil, which is distraction, going through the motions without really living. It's also what I call the difference between the historical Jesus and the inner Christ.

"It's important to distinguish between the external and inner Christ. The former is the self-declared guardian of what is perceived as the only truth - the head mind. The latter is a call and striving toward an inner truth, that is authentic only in the way that it is lived - what I call the heart mind.

"You can go through the motions of religious ritual but it will merely be an external exercise of the head mind if you don't discover your own meaningful truth within that ritual.

"For centuries, the guardian has been dominant, emphasizing what separates us, intolerant of other beliefs, self-righteously seeking to forcibly convert, arguing and fighting over the literal meaning of words. It's the root of all fanaticism and mutates into evil. All sense of humanity gets lost when it comes to dealing with the non-believer.

"The one that is awakened to the inner Christ is first and foremost a disciple and servant of life and aligned with soul purpose. The other by principle has a negative outlook of man as weak and sinful, keeping him in fear of a vengeful God waiting to pass sentence. It is separation from soul purpose that produces negative emotions such as hatred, fear and anxiety.

"And so, the one keeps us behind the veil by holding our attention to the external, while the heart awakens gradually to that new reality.

"And at the start of that path the hardest part is to seize control over your thoughts, your wishes and senses.

"The inner voice, your intuition, will only be heard when you silence the cacophony of external voices. Looking inward means learning to see without eyes, hear without ears, walk without feet, touch and feel without using your hands..."

We arrived in Santa Cilia late in the afternoon, the sky darkening and the first raindrops falling. Greta was waiting for us in the hostel.

"At last! I've been waiting for you guys. Want to join me for a beer?"

She gave us a warm hug. It had been a slow, lonely walk for her from Jaca to Santa Cilia, "but in a way my best day so far," she beamed.

A friendly Spanish lady from the village prepared a meal for the small group of pilgrims in the hostel and stamped our credentials. (*The credential, successor to the original document given to the pilgrims during the Middle Ages, is a document, certifying the hiker as a pilgrim, recording the passage through locations along the Camino.*) Together with a Brazilian couple, who joined us, we enjoyed spaghetti Bolognese, salad and a Rioja red wine.

Greta related her dream. "I seldom remember dreams. But this dream I do remember. I woke up at about 4 in the morning. I was walking the path, the same old Roman path I walked today. The cobblestones were askew. It was dark and rainy. I was having trouble

walking and swearing at myself for having come this
long way to walk the Camino. Then I hear this clear,
beautiful voice:

'Greta, this is a holy path. Be mindful. Treat it with
respect.'

"Then the sun burst through the clouds, lighting the
path ahead of me as if there were a fire burning in the
background, so strong was the light. And then this wave
of energy hits me. I get dressed and start my walk. I'll
get to Santiago. I'm healthy and strong enough to do it."

Chuck smiled. "It's your initiation. Our Swedish lady
has her Viking energy back."

"Yes, Viking energy. Thank you, Chuck. Ya Hoo!
Let's drink to that."

We downed another bottle of Rioja. It was a welcome
relief to have a bed after having spent the previous night
sleeping outdoors and not knowing whether we would be
drenched by a sudden rainfall.

It rained heavily all night and the rain had not stopped
when we left the hostel the next morning. We donned
our rain gear. Chuck trudged ahead in a long raincoat,
carrying a staff that really did make him look like one of
those medieval pilgrims eternalized in the form of
statues and symbols along the path.

A group of elderly women mumbled prayers and
wished a 'buen Camino' making the sign of the cross by
touching forehead, chest, shoulder left and then right.
Wishing a pilgrim 'buen Camino' or a good road is the
form of greeting deeply ingrained in every village and

town on the Camino, its deeper meaning being a recognition, a sign of respect, and a blessing of the pilgrim taking on the hardship of a journey in search of deeper meaning.

It was a prayer, a mantra that every pilgrim wished a fellow pilgrim along the way, passing on the blessing hundreds, thousands and millions of times. I asked Chuck about it sometime later. "It's about embracing the path of the disciple, greeting the inner Christ of your fellow pilgrim on the path of life. In the Asian tradition, they call it namaste, meaning I bow to you from heart to heart in a sign of respect and a cure for the obstacle of pride."

The path from Santa Cilia to the mountain top village of Artieda was a long meandering one with cornfield after cornfield. Judging from the odd remaining stonewall enclosures, it was obvious that the fields had once been subdivided smaller patches that gave way to mass agriculture. It was a complete contrast to the beautiful walk from the monastery San Juan de la Pena the day before, and I began counting the hours it would take us to reach Artieda. The Camino was again teaching me one of life's lessons: There were beautiful sunny days and miserable rainy ones.

Life was about dealing with and accepting the impermanence of both light and shadow, joy and sadness, birth and death, illness and health. Clinging to a no longer existent past or a yet undefined future was part of the self-created obstacle that prevented real living in the here and now. So, I guess I just had to accept the rainy day and the cold wind blowing against my face, and my bones shaking from the cold.

The pebble-strewn path went up a hilly incline where I noticed a somewhat ramshackle SEAT car rolling to a stop. The gray sky loomed like a heavy mantle, with light clouds interspersed between dark rain clouds.

A priest got out of the car and waved to us from the distance. Then, holding a cross above his head he sank to his knees, gently placing it on the path in front of him. Gradually the landscape changed. We moved closer to the mountains, passing the villages of Martes and Mianos tucked into the hillside on the left, until we reached the old Roman pathway that led up the summit to Artieda. There we found the hostel amid beautifully restored old homes close to the medieval church of St. Martin.

The village dates back to the Roman era and was part of the Leyre monastery until at least 919 A.D. We had decided to have our light evening meal of cheese, olives and red wine at a spot overlooking the valley below.

Meanwhile it had stopped raining and a beautiful rainbow could be seen stretching over the valley, where the Aragon river wound its way into the Yesa reservoir. The yellow evening light spotlighted the old stone houses in an orange-red hue.

Several slogans could be seen on the walls of the houses: "Aqui Hay Vida – Yesa No"

"It means 'Here there is life, no to Yesa'," said Juan, a soft-spoken, yet energetic young man with short-cropped hair and beard who had joined us. It emerged that he was an active member of the protest movement against the Yesa dam project which would flood the entire valley below us.

"One of the oldest part of the Camino that you will walk tomorrow, lovely forest and meadows, all will be underwater. We are fighting on, while every day they are building that dam wall higher, and for what? Irrigation for monoculture crops that we don't need."

The project was essentially about heightening the existing dam wall - built in 1959 - by more than half to increase the volume of the Yesa reservoir to irrigation the Bardenas area and provide drinking water for the city of Zaragoza.

But of far greater concern to Juan and his protest movement was the detection of a landslide on the flank of the dam site that had already led to problems during the original construction of the reservoir.

"Further landslides have just recently been detected. We are really worried that the dam will not be able to withstand the pressure and that the earth will give way, flooding the town of Sanguesa with its more than 5,000 people and that is why we are fighting this project."

Chuck described it as part of a bigger problem of human consciousness, and the rule of cause and effect.

"We have become alienated from Earth, from creation. We see ourselves as separate from Mother Earth, without realizing that we are a part of her and that how we treat her is actually how we treat ourselves."

"You have a point," Greta said. "I do see that we exploit and poison the soils with pesticides. We destroy the rainforest and replace it with geneticallymanipulated monoculture. We poison the air by burning fossil fuels. But are we all responsible. I've tried to live a good life, going into organic and all that, and I still got cancer. I feel punished by God. I did everything right, I thought."

"That's not how you should see it," Chuck said in his most gentle and understanding tone of voice.

"God, or creation, call it what you like, does not punish. Pain and suffering is a consequence of collective action.

"I would be the last person to blame you or anyone else for getting cancer. Health is largely a personal responsibility, but illness sometimes strikes at random and then the issue is one of deep individual transformation and soul-searching."

At this point we were interrupted by music blaring from the main town square. "You must join us for the party," Juan suggested. "It's our chocolate festival. The women in town come gather to cook chocolate, and you must come and taste some."

The townspeople were celebrating, dancing in the streets and having fun.

Firecrackers cut through the air as if the town itself were rising up to drive away the demons threatening its way of life.

"Making a noise is part of our culture," Juan said before we retired for bed well before midnight.

We were tired pilgrims needing sleep. But we didn't get much of it that night. The party was still in full swing when we took to the road just after 7:30 a.m.

CHAPTER SIX — DESERTED VILLAGES

On the horizon, the Yesa reservoir shimmered in dazzling green-blue light, reminiscent of a picture-postcard from a Caribbean resort. Those tentacles would one day spread and flood forever the same ancient path we were walking on.

Each of us walked with a feeling of nostalgia and sadness.

We felt the need to have time alone when we left Artieda. It was not something we had discussed, but just happened as we all walked at our own pace, reflecting on the processes within that needed time for calibration.

We agreed to meet again at the Albergue hostel in the village of Ruesta.

The path took us into a beautiful forest, the ancient trees folding their branches over us and forming a protective tunnel. Swarms of flies chased me on until I reached an opening.

A protest sign over a mound of rock again reminded us that this place of beauty where pilgrims had walked for centuries, would soon be no more.

The ruins of the chapel of San Juan Bautista were all that remained of the monastery of San Juan de Maltray.

From the slabs of stone that had fallen from the wall a pilgrim had formed a cross on the floor, pointing to the altar, where a crucifix had been placed inside a wreath woven from grass.

After another half hour of walking the ruins of Ruesta loomed on a hilltop. The village was deserted in 1959 when the inhabitants were forced to move after construction of the Yesa reservoir that flooded their farmland below.

My guide book told me that the castle to the west was of Arab origin and dated back to the 10th century, while to the east stood the 16th- century Iglesia Santa Maria church.

During the Middle Ages, Ruesta was not only an important meeting place for pilgrims but also home to the oldest Jewish quarter in the province of Aragon.

On the way toward the village I met Francois, who was walking the Camino with two donkeys in tow. One of the animals was limping and needed attention. I wondered why someone would walk the Camino with two donkeys and he told me his story.

A few months ago, his 45-year-old daughter had died of cancer. She had made plans to walk the Camino with a donkey, but the cancer was faster. During the final hours of her life, the father had made a pledge:

"I will find a donkey and do that walk for you."

She died soon afterwards at peace in his arms.

The young couple running the hostel in Ruesta made us a delicious bocadillo sandwich for lunch.

Two elderly men sat down for coffee after visiting the Iglesia de Santa Maria. We learned later that they were former inhabitants. Most of the village was out of bounds because of the danger of collapsing walls.

Roofs of once noble homes had collapsed. Efforts were under way to restore some of the beautiful old buildings but the signs of decay were evident, the weeds and undergrowth showing as little disregard for heritage as the politicians and corporations responsible for the Yesa project.

"I find this all too depressing. I don't know about you guys, but I'm not in the mood to stay in a dead village overnight. It's like the ghosts of sad people are all around us," Greta said pulling up her backpack.

"I have to stay a few days to give my donkeys some rest. And there is nothing rushing me," Francois said.

Our next stop was Undues de Lerda. A winding, steep path led us out of Ruesta.

Greta was in a somber mood, her feet trudging heavily with each step, seemingly pulling her into a deeper abyss.

"I'm sorry, guys," she gasped. "I think I'm falling into another one of my depressions. Don't take it personally. That deserted old town, the dam project, how we humans are treating the Earth all somehow make me feel so incredibly sad, and I know this feeling too well. I'm so frustrated. I've tried so many things – therapies, medication, mediation and now this walk on the Camino..."

"What is depression? Nobody really has an answer," Chuck interjected. "We have some doctor interpreting it as a problem with the brain's serotonin and gives medication to relieve you of your pain.

"Then you go to a therapist, who sees your condition as an emotional response to some negative experience in your life, and you delve into that past experience. Then you find that doesn't really work and go to see a psychologist who tells you it is all a result of your faulty thinking and that you should re-programme yourself by thinking positive.

"After a while you find someone who tells you it is all the result of the society you live in with its inequality, while the eco-therapist out in the boondocks tells you it's because you've lost contact with nature and your true self.

"All of them fall prey to their own expertise, one side claiming that it's all because of some malfunction in brain chemistry, and the other that it's because our mind is focusing too much on the negative due to some past experience."

"What if everyone has found a bit of the truth?" I asked.

"Isn't it the same with religion and all other belief systems? Greta asked. "Some people are saying you have to make a pilgrimage to Mecca, others that you have to meditate long enough to gain enlightenment, and others that you have to abide by the commandments and the teachings of Jesus."

"Yeah, in principle you can make everything into a religion," Chuck responded.

"By proclaiming something that you believe to be the truth. Thinking from within a box. You define four walls and remain in there without climbing out and seeing the bigger picture, which is far more vast and complex than you ever imagined possible.

"Let's get back to what you call your depression, Greta. You've been seeking the answer from outside, hoping that some therapist leads you to a magic answer and solves your problem.

"You're saying all these therapies are useless?" I asked.

"Not at all. Let me tell you a story. In life, there are problems and there are difficulties. In most cases we are dealing with difficulties and not problems.

"There is this very wealthy lady with everything life has to offer who goes to a therapist, and tells him. 'I think I have a depression. I'm so unhappy. Life is so meaningless.' The therapist looks at her and then calls in his Mexican cleaning lady, who tells the wealthy lady her story.

"The cleaning lady says she lost her husband and three children in a car accident. She is walking the streets and thinks that life is over for her. When she gets home she finds a hungry stray cat outside her door and gives it a little milk. The cat jumps into her lap, purring and showing its appreciation. From that day she decides to give something to someone in need every day, a hot cup of coffee to the homeless man, helping an elderly woman cross a street. By selflessly doing something for someone each day, the Mexican woman gradually loses all her sadness in the knowledge that there are always folks out there carrying a much heavier burden and needing help.

"The wealthy woman has tears flowing down her cheeks, realizing instantly how immensely fortunate she is and how well life has treated her.

"But there is this world out there with its regular propaganda messages telling us: You have to be happy. If you aren't smiling and happy, then something is wrong with you. So, what do we see out here?"

"Nothing but a lonely path going up a valley and down a valley," I remarked "Can't wait to get to the next village to have a cold beer."

"I get your point," Greta said, giving us an intense look of relief."

"You go up a hill and you go down a hill. You have happy moments and sad moments. You have day and you have night."

"Exactly. Its finding your own meaning and ways of just dealing with life's fluctuations, staying in the moment in the knowledge that yes … this moment, too, shall pass."

I listened to Chuck's words, seeing the long road still ahead, feeling exhausted, my body aching and perspiring from the heat.

All that kept me going was the thought of sitting outside a bar enjoying that cold beer.

The village of Undues de Lerda was a distant silhouette on the horizon.

CHAPTER SEVEN — FIELD OF STARS

There was a mystical whisper of silence in the air.

Shooting stars streaked over the village of Undues de Lerda as we made ourselves comfortable in the square outside the Ermita de Santa Quiteria, chapel.

"When you see a shooting star, you should make a wish. But just don't tell anyone. It should be a special wish just for you," Greta said. "I'm really enjoying this time with you guys," she added as we dug into the cheese and red wine.

"It's often that you see shooting stars on the Camino, but today is very special, very unusual," said a man who introduced himself as Arturo from Madrid. I imagined him a teacher or lecturer – the "mad professor," a water bottle dangling loosely from his pot belly, and a map in a plastic bag hung on a string around his neck.

He had arrived at the Albergue hostel just before us, and apart from him, we were the only pilgrims in the spacious new building.

Arturo told us that the name Santiago de Compostella

could literally be translated to 'Field of Stars'. It was around the year 900 A.D. when a shepard called Pelagius witnessed a shower of shooting stars.

This continued for several nights. Intrigued by the phenomenon, he followed the path of the shooting stars to the hilltop where it was said that St. James and two of his disciples, Theodorus and Athanasius, had been buried in unmarked graves.

There Pelagius began digging, and uncovered the remains of the three men in what was part of a larger Roman place of burial.

After much consultation and prayer with the local bishop it was finally determined that they were indeed the remains of St. James, Apostle of Jesus, and the two other disciples.

Since then, the hilltop where today we find the cathedral of Santiago has been known as the field of stars – campo de estrellas – where the stars fell.

"The heavenly shower of stars that led to the rediscovery of the grave of St. James is the actual link between the destination of the Camino and the stars," Arturo said waving his hands as he pointed to the sky above.

"But isn't this all a legend – like many of the other stories we hear on the Camino? Greta asked.

"Of course, you can dismiss all these "legends" due to a lack of hard historical evidence. But as the saying goes: If one believes, no proof is necessary, and if one does not believe, no proof is sufficient, "Chuck replied.

"To the ancient peoples, the heavenly directions were of great importance, especially the east where the sun rises. It was seen as the place of hope and resurrection of Christ.

"That is why the churches face east. The west, where the sun sets, is the place of death and of the past," Chuck added, continuing his explanation:

"The Milky Way we see in all its splendor shows the path of the human soul. Just as the sun reveals the path during the day, the stars show us the way at night.

"Now obviously only a few pilgrims would have walked the path at night because of the dangers of being assaulted by robbers or attacked by wild animals.

"The way of the stars was meant more as a symbol of the path through life, with paradise being found at the end of life at the end of the earth – Finisterre – a walk from the old life, the past in the west, to a new, cleansed future in the east.

"That's a nice way of putting it," Greta said. "I like the idea of walking to the end at Finisterre.".

"We look down upon the people of the past, but look at what they created," Arturo said gesticulating, for greater emphasis and his face getting more flushed as he talked. "Magnificent cathedrals lasting for generations, for centuries, with fantastic works of art. Show me any building today that will last for the next hundred years."

"True," Chuck added. "The difference is that mankind was then embedded in a cosmic and spiritual order. Many of the towns and cities were built like a mandala, with the place of worship in the center. Special trees and places in nature were revered. We seem to have lost something on the way.

"Mundane things of everyday life are what make the difference. We ridicule the Muslims for prostrating themselves five times a day to pray to Mecca. But look at the compound effect over a lifetime. Or take the Buddhist who prays the mantra 'om mani padme hum' 108 times a day. That's a lot of good energy that is created."

"We should look more often at the stars. How small we are when we look at this giant cosmos spread out above us," Greta said taking another swig from her wine.

Chuck and Arturo went on a long discussion lasting well after midnight on the effects of the planets and their resonating effects on all of life. What I understood was that science was making great headway in confirming what ancient peoples knew all along:

Energy waves emanating from the sun, the moon and the other planets with profound effect on all living beings.

Every planet seems to have its own particular rhythm that resonates with the cells of our body. In turn every cell in an organism has its own resonance that forms a matrix of sound with the cosmos. Everything is in movement and in resonance, which is why we need to be mindful of the negative resonances that disturb the sensitive energy field of the body.

What I learned that night was that the ancient teachers had great knowledge of the healing effects of rhythm and sound on the body. Chuck was the opinion that the intonation of the syllable 'om' was universal and in direct resonance with the sun, its origins found deep in the collective mind rather than in a particular religion.

Voicing the syllable made energy move all the way from the lower abdomen, up the spinal cord and into the brain.

All the great mantras and prayers in the ancient languages, be they in Sanskrit, Aramaic or Latin, put particular emphasis on certain vowels that resonated with certain body organs.

We would start practicing them the next day, and I was completely open to that experiment.

CHAPTER EIGHT — LIVING

Arturo struggled with a massive backpack. He probably had half a library stashed in his bag, I thought. I was about to comment on why he didn't empty it to make life easier when Chuck stopped me with a wink.

"Interfere only when asked. It may be that he needs to find out for himself.

"You would not have been the first pilgrim to have commented on his bag and to what effect – just wasted energy."

Arturo had hogged the conversation the night before and I felt a little aggressive toward him. Who was this intellectual snob, fresh on the Camino for only a couple of days, trying to tell us everything about it? He should walk a couple of weeks before talking so much.

I was quick to get away from him. I remembered how I had started, shedding my own heavy load and exchanging my broken, heavy backpack for a much smaller one. Shedding the clutter both mentally and physically was part of the process.

I shared my thoughts with Greta, who compared it to aging. "My mother lived in this big house surrounded by the furniture collected over a lifetime," she said.

"There was my father's study exactly the way it was when he died 20 years ago, the rooms in which we had grown up, almost unchanged. But there comes a point where you cannot physically cope and keeping such a big place clean and in shape. She had to make the hard decision to move to an old-age home, where she's spending the last years of her life in a little room with a bed, a table and a few sentimental belongings, pondering on those things that are gone and no more.

"Isn't it strange that when it comes down to it, material things lose their shine? I would choose an experience like walking the Camino any day over spending my money on a new bedroom suite. Do you still remember the things you bought 10, 20 years ago?"

Greta had a point, and my mind went back to the life I had lived before starting my walk. A life of slavery working an unsatisfying job with most of my pay going to pay off a mortgage, cars, electronic gadgets and other stuff that I believed were essential for my well-being.

Finally, almost entering middle age, I was just beginning to feel life. This was truly about fully living the ups and down of the here and NOW, hearing birdsong in the distance, seeing the falcon circling in the blue sky, hearing the clack-clack of my hiking boots on the ancient Roman cobblestone path, feeling my heartbeat and inhaling the fresh aroma of wild herbs and flowers along the path, being aware of the positive and negative thoughts that come and go.

I was alone with my thoughts until I reached Sanguesa late morning. This was the town the young man Juan had told us would be flooded if the Yesa reservoir wall broke.

It was the first large settlement in the Navarra province with the 13th-century Palacio del Principe de Viana, formerly a residence of the kings, and the Palacio de Vallesantoro. The most significant religious building, the Iglesia de Santa Maria la Real was indicative of the importance to the medieval pilgrim movement.

At the entrance of the town's 13th or 14th century Iglesia de Santiago was an impressive figure of St. James in a red robe with an image of two pilgrims kneeling on either side.

After my little round of sightseeing, I finally found Chuck and Greta in a bar just off the Iglesia de Santa Maria la Real. Greta looked pale, after an exhausting walk in the heat.

"I'm sorry, I will have to do without you guys for the rest of the day. I'm taking the bus to Izco. I just can't walk for today."

We accompanied Greta to the bus stop and agreed that she should not be out walking with us on a day where temperatures where already soaring over the 30 degrees Celsius (86 Fahrenheit) and we had a steep climb up the Alto de Aibar mountain ahead of us.

I left Sanguesa half an hour after Chuck, following the path out of town past a huge protest sign on the hillside to the left with the words: "Yesa No."

I tried to banish from my mind the image of this beautiful town with its lovely palaces and churches flooded by a wall of water gushing down the valley. If I was afraid, how must the people living in the town feel.

The steep path followed a river bank. To the right were the ruins of Saint Bartolomé, the first Francisan monastery founded on the Iberian Peninsula. The saint was said to have resided in the monastery while on his pilgrimage to Santiago in the years 1213 to 1215.

I made a mental note to ask Arturo about the story that the saint struck the ground nearby with his walking stick, where a mulberry tree grew, that although dried up, still has bark with healing properties.

The heat wave forced me to make a stop at the Fuenta de San Francisco, or fountain of Saint Francis. It was a welcome relief to soak my tired feet in the cold water and refill my water bottles with "saint water."

There was not a single human to be found along the path which took me past vineyards, grain fields and deserted old farmhouses.

The mountain range ahead was crowned by wind turbines, the gentle swishing sound of their rotor blades echoing down below. I regretted not having taken a longer break. I felt my throat contracting and a pain in my chest.

The euphoria, I had felt earlier in the day had given way to a desolate feeling of utter loneliness. I missed Greta and Chuck walking behind or ahead of me. I had become so used to their presence, and it was so comforting just to have them within eyesight.

I was hoping all the while that I would meet Chuck around the next turn, only to find another long, winding steep path ahead. I felt myself getting angry at Chuck for having insisted that we walk the section alone.

In the haze, I saw images of deserted villages, their inhabitants decimated by the plague, decaying bodies being eaten by ravens and other birds of prey.

I saw myself trundling along as one of the last survivors, searching for the last morsels to eat.

Death could be a very lonely affair. You come into the world alone with one inhalation and you leave the world alone with one exhaling breath.

Only if you are lucky might you have a loved one holding your hand.

Meanwhile, my water supply was dwindling. I forced myself to keep going, making my mind think positive.

Finally, I reached the summit, with a spectacular view of the town of Monreal in the distance. The feelings of desperation and loneliness dissipated.

After passing through a forest of young pine trees, I came upon a herd of cattle and found myself conversing with the gentle animals, the bells around their necks chiming in different tones and melodies.

I made it into Izco just before sunset where I found Greta and Chuck out on the terrace of the Albergue hostel.

I was overjoyed to see them again, and fell into their arms, quite unlike my normally reserved nature.

We went to bed early, wanting to leave before sunrise the next day. My sleep was restless and haunted by bad dreams. I dreamed I was walking on muddy ground, my feet getting stuck, my legs giving way under the heavy weight of a backpack.

I was walking through deserted village after deserted village. It was as if mankind had been eradicated from the Earth by the plague and I was the lone surviving human being, desperately searching for some sign of life.

Cows with swollen udders were bleating in pain, and with the rotting body of a herdsman was leaning against a tree stump.

There was the smell of rot and decay in the air, but the faster I tried to walk, the deeper my feet sank into the mud until I was stuck up the hip, having to force myself to continue but losing energy and willpower.

I woke up from the nightmare, my body sweating and my heart beating against my chest in a quick staccato rhythm.

CHAPTER NINE — INNER PEACE

That morning I found myself looking at a different person in the mirror. My eyes were bloodshot, my face swollen.

"You look terrible," Greta said, looking at me with some concern. I shared my dream with my two companions.

Chuck's theory was that I had come under the influence of a morphic resonance in a field charged with traumatic events during the plague of the Middle Ages.

"You must look at it like a compact disc with information etched to it. The Earth, the plants, the human beings that once lived there, and something in your consciousness picked up that energy field.

"Some scholars would even have us believe that we are governed and controlled by these unseen forces," Chuck said.

"Accessing certain morphogenic fields has a lot to do with your state of mind. So I'm asking you what was your state of mind when you had that feeling you were walking through a plague-hit medieval village more than 500 years ago?"

"Loneliness. I was feeling terribly alone, maybe even angry at the world. I don't know really."

"The Camino is a holy path. I firmly believe that," Chuck said, adjusting his backpack for our good eight hour walk to Puenta la Reina that day.

"Where there is much light you will also find much darkness. We have to be aware of our thoughts and emotions all the time. It's our demons of fear, anger, frustration that we need to defeat or they will take control. Have a mind of peace, love and compassion, you will go into resonance with the beauty and peace around you. You need to detox, my friend."

I was at a loss and needed help, both on a physical and emotional level.

It was the day I learned the Buddhist mantra: om mani padme hum, which even for non-Buddhists has a very powerful healing effect in purifying the dark emotions that have taken hold.

Chuck explained to us that the syllable om was the universal sound and could be compared to the All-Existence, going into resonance with God and the world, dissolving the mind into the purity of body and spirit. Humming "om" was the first syllable at the beginning of the mantra and set the tone for mani padme, the jewel in the lotus flower, which stirred the love and compassion in our heart. The ending with the powerful hum in the lower belly took us back into the unity of our true nature, our higher self, our intuition and inner wisdom.

We left Itzco in single file, repeating om mani padme hum over and over, along endless kilometers of unpopulated areas. Our humming of the mantra was interspersed only by the calls of the griffon vultures from the canyons of Foz de Lumbier and Foz de Arbayun and the many other birds in the area.

It occurred to me that such prayers hummed hundreds of millions of times by pilgrims over the centuries and the buen camino greeting were very powerful etchings of light onto the morphogenic field. Was this why the Camino, the cathedrals, Lourdes and many other holy places acted like a magnet for people seeking comfort and solace?

If you opened your heart to the magic, this powerful energy could be felt with every step on the way. I remembered again my good friend Claire's words of advice before my departure:

"Remain humble on the path, or the path will humble you."

In my euphoria en route to Sanguesa I had become judgmental about pilgrims such as Arturo, thought of myself as being further down the road and become too over-confident. Once again, I was being taught a lesson in humility.

Yes, I had to tell myself, everyone has their own demons to deal with. Every pilgrim walks the Camino for different reasons. Some do it just for the sporting challenge, others for deep soul searching and yet others for no particular reasons.

Nobody could really look into the soul of another

person and to judge how far down the path they were.
Sometimes, only sometimes, there was an inkling of the
pains, joys, obstacles, fears and challenges the person
had gone through before meeting you at a certain point
in time. So, my friend, just be tolerant …om mani padme
hum.

Every pilgrim gives to the path his or her hopes,
wishes, and prayers or, just accepts things the way they
are. The senses are sharpened as you walk like a tiger,
long kept in a cage, that starts rediscovering its natural
instincts when released again into the jungle. The
problems you came with start dissolving with every step
you take moving forward and leaving things behind. The
pains that we have inflicted on others and that have been
inflicted on us are left behind like the lost dreams,
unfulfilled promises and disappointments.

Everything is transformed into the here and now.
These issues that have tied us to one spot and kept us
from moving forward on the soul's path become
irrelevant. Tensions that have manifested themselves in
the body begin to dissolve, so that a meeting with the
true inner self becomes possible.

I came over the hilltop, the church of Santa Maria de
Eunate loomed ahead in the open countryside. This was
one of the most unique and beautiful buildings I had seen
so far on the Camino.

It is surrounded by an artistic corral of stone with 33
archways decorated with figures having animal and
human features. The origins of the building remain a
mystery.

Some writers date it back to the Knights Templar of the 12th century because of its similarities to the Church of the Holy Sepulchre in Jerusalem.

The octagonal shape of the inner complex, with a five-cornered exterior and an circular apse, give the place a special energy

As we entered the building, its narrow alabaster windows and the candlelight filling the room gave it a mystical aura.

The Madonna was sitting on a throne with the Christ on her lap, her hands gently reaching out.

I closed my eyes, suddenly feeling overwhelmed by thousands of pin-sized light particles pouring down me.

The Madonna, on her Seat of Wisdom, reached out to me in a communion of the heart and I felt warm tears rolling down my cheeks.

CHAPTER TEN — CROSSROADS

The town of Puenta la Reina, "Bridge of the Queen," is named after an elegant 11th-century bridge spanning the Arga river. The Calle Mayor main street took us through the old part of town straight across the bridge.

As the story goes, it was the wish of the Queen, the widow of Sancho Garces III, to have the bridge built, creating the foundation of a booming economic and social life in the town. Puenta la Reina is also where two Camino paths meet: the Camino Frances, starting from the French town of St.-Jean-Pied-de-Port and the Camino Aragonese.

After encountering only, a handful of pilgrims on the Camino Aragonese, we were stunned by the masses of backpacking pilgrims pouring into the Calle Mayor from the Camino Frances. The Camino Aragonese had such solitude that at times the solitude itself was almost like noise.

As we had spent some time in the Santa Maria de Eunate it was dark by the time we reached the first Albergue hostel in Puenta la Reina. It was completely filled. We eventually found a hotel, happy to enjoy a little comfort after roughing it in the mass accommodations of the hostels the previous days. Each of us had a room with a large comfortable bed and bathroom, and we had ample space to do the washing for the day and hang our clothing from the balcony to dry.

Later we found our friend Arturo in one of the restaurants along the Calle Mayor digging into a large piece of steak and huge portion of French fries. We chose the menu del dia with a big salad, paella and desert with a label bottle of wine included. Arturo confided to us why he was walking the Camino, talking of "we" instead of "I."

"We need to rediscover our Christian roots so that Islam does not swallow us. We have this problem that we are losing the roots of our traditions, culture and religion," he said, taking another big bite from his steak.

"Organized religion has not been particularly attractive, if you ask me," I interjected. "Boring sermons with theology nobody understands anymore.

"For centuries, the Church has portrayed God as a punishing God if you misbehave. The Church has manipulated its followers into treading a narrow path of joyless obedience. Non-believers were excluded as heathens who could be persecuted, slaughtered in wars and enslaved."

Arturo went into a long lecture on how Islam was doing precisely that. "We have lived peacefully with the Muslims here in Spain for a long time. But something is changing. Oil money is financing big new mosques and we don't know what the Imams are teaching behind those closed walls. We are non-believers to them, and they don't believe in dialogue and peaceful co-existence. It's time that we woke up to see what is happening around us.

"Our way of life and culture is being threatened by these people. I tell you they have a plan to make all of Europe, all of the world, Islam and it's been like that since the days of Mohammed.

Arturo's face became redder and redder as he spoke, his blood pressure rising.

"I don't think we would see them as a threat if we felt secure in our own belief system," Chuck said.

"So, tell me what you believe!"

At this point we were interrupted by a middle-aged woman. She was dressed in a dirty black robe, holding out her hands for us to give her money and moaning with sadness.

Arturo gestured at her to leave us alone, saying something in Spanish that made her respond angrily with a flurry of hissing, spitting and other guttural utterances. I was taken aback by the dark, fiery look in her eyes.

"Gypsies," he said. "These are organized gangs that come to steal, rob and beg. There will be a man around the corner collecting all the money she has gotten from begging."

"Even if it's true, we are assuming. That was a bit hard. It would not have hurt us have given her a little something," Greta said.

Our conversation stopped. There was a long moment of uncomfortable silence, with Chuck closing his eyes in deep concentration. Then, wiping his forehead, he said:

"Here we are talking about faith and God and look at what we get confronted with.

"There is a difference between religion and spirituality. Religion is a belief in a certain faith, ritual or personal God. Spirituality is broad and undefined, giving room for personal choice and a constant search for broader meaning."

"You see that is where we differ," Arturo blurted out. "I think we need orientation on God's word in the Bible, and to follow practices like going to Mass and know what is right and wrong as set out in the commandments."

"Well, if you want to see the Bible as God's word, then there is much room for interpretation here," Chuck argued. "Just go back to the fourth century when Emperor Constantine I asked 12 bishops to work out a common doctrinal orthodoxy at the Council of Nicea. Everything deemed pagan or heresy, like the Gospel of St. Thomas that man should seek the Kingdom of God within himself and on Earth excluded.

"The genuine teachings of Jesus to follow one's soul path to become a "son of God" through radical personal transformation and growth was changed into the belief that only Christ was God, who brought about the salvation of humanity in his sacrifice for their sins by dying on the cross.

"The term Christ, or "Christos" from the Greek,

means the anointed or the one, chosen to spread certain teachings. Since the fourth century, the entire focus of the Church in the religious sense has been on the sacrificial aspect of the Crucifixion.

"The ideology as decreed by the Council of Nicea henceforth became the official teaching of the Church, with other teachings going underground. It led to the creation of a monstrous Roman papal bureaucracy that still exists today.

"In truth, the teachings of Jesus are about the resurrection or mystical rebirth of the soul to higher consciousness. Jesus was a storyteller talking in parables and aphorisms that left room for interpretation and individual imagery, speaking to those going through life with their eyes open but seeing nothing and their ears open but understanding nothing of what they hear."

Arturo argued that doctrine provided orientation and a firm grounding to humanity seeking a meaning for life. "What I hear from you is esoteric speculation, so why don't we just agree that we differ fundamentally?" With that, Arturo excused himself, while we took a slow walk back to our hotel.

Chuck was not feeling well. The next morning, he awoke with a fever. He looked so bad that Greta and I strongly advised, that we call a doctor. He told us he would be fine and just needed a day or two of rest.

We had admired the man's physical fitness and the ease with which he accomplished the daily stages on the Camino of up to 30 kilometers and more. I started feeling guilty — maybe we had all pushed each other too hard. Chuck, after all was a man in his late 60s.

But it was more than just physical exhaustion. Something seemed to have taken hold of him and was draining all his energy. Greta spent much of the morning bringing Chuck hot tea with honey and ginger, finding a pharmacy and getting medication for what we thought was a bad bout of influenza. But by late morning, when there was still no sign of improvement, Greta became adamant: "I'm calling a doctor."

He was there within half an hour. The doctor diagnosed an irregular heart beat and told us that Chuck needed to be taken to hospital for further examination. Chuck was having none of it. "Nobody is taking me to a hospital!"

"Only at your own risk;" the doctor said. "I can't force you."

We agreed that we would call him immediately if the condition worsened.

At some point in the afternoon Chuck's condition improved. He asked us to accompany him to the Iglesia de Santiago, a church in the center of town with a monumental doorway of Moorish architectural design.

Chuck led us to a stone-carved figure holding a snake. "And I saw three unclean spirits like frogs come out of the mouth of the dragon. Protection, light, transformation."

We did not understand Chuck's quote from Revelations and his mumblings of several other biblical passages.

Greta and I exchanged puzzled looks, thinking that the fever must have led to some type of delirium.

We lit candles at the altar and then accompanied Chuck back to the hotel. "Remember the old lady beggar from yesterday?"

I felt a cold shudder run down my spine. I remembered the dark, angry look in the woman's eyes, and her spitting on the ground as she left us. It had been something decidedly sinister and evil.

CHAPTER ELEVEN — FEAR

Greta left the next day for Estella on the Camino Frances. It was sad to say goodbye to a good friend.

"I think you guys need some time alone," she said as we parted. "We will see each other."

We had a problem saying goodbye. It was a last brief hug, a wave and that was it. Chuck and I were now alone with our thoughts in the bus to Unquera on the Camino del Norte, also known as the coastal route. Should we have stayed with Greta out of a sense of responsibility?

We put the thought aside. As much as bonds between pilgrims grew on the Camino, the path was also very much a path of individual self-discovery and self-development.

The Camino del Norte would not be without its own challenges, and we would at times be in remote and unmarked territory. From Unquera it was another 468 kilometers to Santiago, the route joining the Camino Frances again in the town of Melide. From there it was only a two-day walk to our final destination — Santiago.

But the plan was that we would take the Camino Primitivo from Oviedo — a lonely challenging route through the mountains of Asturias and the towns of Salas, Tineo, A Fonsagrada, Lugo and then Melide.

The Camino del Norte and the Camino Primitivo are often described as the original route. News that the grave of St. James had been found spread rapidly in Europe around the ninth century. Because most of Spain was occupied by Muslims, the Christian pilgrims were forced to take the coastal route, starting along the French-Spanish border and moving across the Basque country, Cantabria, Asturias and Galicia.

After the Arab invasion of the Iberian Peninsula in 711, the last pockets of Christian resistance could be found in the mountains. They regrouped under Pelayo, who managed to defeat the first Arab army at Covadonga in the Asturian mountains, establishing the independent kingdom of Asturias.

King Alphonse then confirmed the discovery of the remains of St. James in Santiago, establishing the pilgrimage route between Oviedo and Santiago and securing it for pilgrims.

As in those ancient times, each day on the Camino is a walk into the unknown with a lesson to be learned. Chuck would often tell me that it was a "fasttrack run to self-development that we call life."

Walking so close to the coast, we often saw the weather change within a short period of time. One hour we would be walking in hot sunshine, followed by clouds and rainfall. We would find ourselves along a beautiful path overlooking the ocean, and then on a busy road with heavy-duty trucks, powering past us, the gusts of wind almost blowing us off the road. One night we would be sleeping in a comfortable, private hostel the next in a moldy room with water dripping from the ceiling.

In one of the remote villages between Llanes and Ribadesella, Chuck led us through an alleyway to a hostel run by a charming couple named Ramon and Maria, where Chuck had stayed several times before.

"Qué bueno verte, Chuck! Que trajo un amigo también – you brought a friend too," Ramon said, as they met with a warm embrace.

I immediately felt at home. The walls were decorated with paintings, most of them with Camino motifs. This was a couple that lived for the Camino and loved every visit by a stranger, whom they often met only once and would probably never see again. There are not many people who exude all-encompassing warm heartedness, and spread a good mood and laughter wherever they go.

As they spoke only Spanish, I was only able to follow the gist of the conversation from a word that fell here and there. Chuck told them where we had met and about the encounter in Puenta la Reina, which prompted Maria to head for the kitchen to cook an herbal broth that she made Chuck drink in one big gulp.

I did not catch much of the rest of the conversation that evening over our meal of pulpo (octopus), French fries and salad with a local red wine.

The room was comfortable but I had a restless sleep,

dreaming that a giant octopus was grabbing my throat with its tentacles. I woke with my heart thumping against my chest with a loud da-dumm, da-dumm, dumm.

We departed with another long warm embrace that next morning that almost felt uncomfortable. Maria wrote something in my credential, that Chuck had to translate:

"Have faith and trust. The path will conquer all fear."

The right words at the right time. There were too many thoughts of my chaotic life, I would have to return to after my walk on the Camino.

"Fear comes from separation, separation from the true purpose of the soul," Chuck said. "Where are you? Fear is an emotion that comes from preoccupation of the head mind with superficial things. Courage and faith come from the heart mind – the deep mind."

"That's so easy to say. Too theoretical for me," I responded. "Where do I start, I wake up every night from nightmares."

"To find the path you must become the path. Fear is basically fear about change, leaving the comfort zone of what we know. The mind is preoccupied with things. These thoughts disturb the spirit. You need to confront your fears, and then you might notice the fears getting smaller as you look at them more closely. Look at that octopus and ask it what it needs, and you will see it getting smaller and smaller as you go along.

"Remember, energy follows thought and energy manifests itself into reality. Where are you? What are you thinking? It's very important to discipline your mind. You create your own reality. You need to take responsibility for what you create. What you think that is what you will become. You decide every day. Am I going to align myself and have a good day or do I get pulled into the maelstrom of other people's energies and distractions?

"First there is intention, then the focus on that intention which brings about the result."

Chuck was good to talk to. I was feeling miserable. The weather was awful and we had to put on slickers before leaving the hostel, our wet boots sank into mud with each step.

"Ritual is a help, and walking the Camino is a ritual," Chuck said, looking at me intently to make sure I was really getting his words.

"When we meditate and really find that space, like the magic moment between inhaling and exhaling, then we are aligned with the deep mind. The empty space between the spokes of the wheel is where you want to be. Let that sink in for a while."

We took a winding path along the coast, through woods, a meadow and then back along the coast. Dark clouds loomed ahead and we managed to reach a lonely chapel just before a heavy downpour.

The Madonna on the altar was especially beautiful, probably sculpted from the image of a young woman in the town. She was holding the baby Jesus close to her breast.

Another veil lifted. Self-recognition was about embracing the inner child, the inner Christ, and finding alignment with the soul purpose. I had to say it out loud facing the ocean on that remote cliff.

"I am centered. I am aligned. Heart and soul are connected and at ONE. I walk from within my center. I fully accept my inner self, my inner child. I fully accept myself in the here and now. I am connected to my soul path, its higher evolution, and in service to the larger WHOLE. I am soul light – I am everlasting light."

CHAPTER TWELVE — THE HOBBIT

The coastal route between Llanes and Ribadesella gave us some beautiful views of the ocean, sunlight penetrating through the darkening clouds, threw its light onto the gentle waves, contrasting with the ragged beachside cliffs that pointed to the sky like jagged, scorched fingers.

On the right bank of the river Bedon we stopped at the picturesque abandoned monastery of San Antolin de Beon, dating back to the early 12th century but probably built on a Celtic place of worship. Legend has it that one Munio Rodriguez wounded a boar and just when he was about to finish it off, it turned on him with a flash of fire coming from its mouth. Rodriquez attributed this to divine intervention and founded the monastery which he dedicated to St. Anthony.

The future saint died at the young age of 35 and was canonized less than a year after his death on June 13, 1231, after excelling as a preacher "with the flash of fire coming from his mouth," a reference to his use of powerful symbolism in Christian scripture.

The place seemed to be haunted by wandering spirits, and as my eyes adjusted to the hazy light, I saw a figure with spidery legs poking around.

"Hola", I shouted, using the Spanish word for hello. But the man was in his own world. From his body movements, he appeared like a hobbit from the pages of J.R.R Tolkien's novel "The Hobbit:" bald head, big eyes and jug ears.

He was counting: "one, two, three ..."

Just before Pineres another rain shower hit us, so by the time we reached the hostel in Ribadesella we were in dire need of drying our wet shoes and clothing.

Several pilgrims had arrived before us, including a gay Austrian couple wearing identical sunglasses and straw hats. They admitted with cheeky smiles that they had taken a taxi to avoid the rain.

An elderly Polish pilgrim who was massaging his aching knees greeting us with a friendly – "dobry wieczór." From what he was able to communicate in a few broken words of English and body language, he had started his pilgrimage in St. Jean and had overcome several obstacles on the way.

Some time later that evening the hobbit arrived, taking the last available bunk bed. He was talking to himself and again counting: "one, one, two, two, three, three ...."

It was a rough night as the hobbit kept rummaging in his plastic shopping bags. At one point shining a flashlight at the gay couple, his eyes almost popping out of his head and spitting the words:

"The day cometh when the wicked and the sinful burn in the eternal lake of fire!"

Someone threw a pillow at the hobbit followed by an incomprehensible flurry of swear words in some foreign language, which made the hobbit duck for cover and pull a blanket over his head, mumbling to himself: "Lake of Fire, Lake of Fire..."

My sleep was interrupted by several loud snorers and dreams in which I was being chased by hobbits in a labyrinth in the cellars of a deserted monastery.

I was wide awake before sunrise, got dressed and left a note for Chuck that I would wait for him in the next village. I needed distance from the hobbit. The guy was a mental case and I wanted no part of that energy around me.

I was in a foul mood, angry and irritable after a bad night's sleep. Why was I doing this – sleeping in a hostel in a bunk bed with 15 other people when I could afford a comfortable bed in a hotel? My body itched and I was sure I had been bitten by some fleas or bed-bugs.

Way down the road I met the Polish guy struggling up a hill, his face red and spittle running from his mouth from exertion. He was supporting himself as best he could with his walking sticks.

"Dzień dobry, buen camino," he panted, a weak smile crossing his lips.

"Buen Camino, good luck!"

Some time later I found an open cafe, and had my first café con leche of the day on a terrace overlooking a river. It didn't take long for Chuck to catch up.

My mood had improved a bit after the second cup of coffee and a cheese and tomato sandwich, and I was happy to see him again.

"Sleeping in the hostels is a lesson in humility," he said guessing my thoughts. It's making do with the basics, cooking and sharing a meal and a room together, sharing the experiences of the day. And, first and foremost, a lesson in tolerance and mindfulness.

"Of course we could be sleeping in a hotel every night and have more sleep. There is no rule saying that you are a good or bad pilgrim if you do one or the other. Just think of it, the guy throwing the pillow at the hobbit..."

It was the trigger, and we burst into such a fit of laughter that my stomach hurt. And there was no holding us when around the corner came the gay Austrians in their straw hats, with the hobbit not far behind, mumbling "one, two, three..."

At Villaviciosa, the path forked. We took the less travelled route that would take us to Oviedo via Valdedios and Pola de Siero on the first stage of the Camino Primitivo.

We passed through several villages with beautiful old horreo granaries built by farmers generations ago on stone pillars capped with staddle stones to prevent rodents from gaining entry.

Near Valdedios we found a beautiful example of Asturian Romanesque architecture with the three naves and a side porch, the chapel of San Salvador de Valdedios, dating back to the ninth century.

The hostel in Pola de Siero was a comfortable old stone house run by a friendly group of hospitaleros in the village. After we had completed our daily routine of handwashing underwear and socks, our Polish pilgrim arrived soon followed, by guess who - the hobbit.

Chuck saw my crestfallen face anticipating another bad night, laughing out aloud at my expense. "You've gone into resonance with this guy. You're trying too hard to avoid him. There's another Camino lesson to be learned here."

"Really funny," I grumbled.

Fortunately he was in a different room this time and we headed for Oviedo the next morning in good spirits – a mere three-hour walk that would take us into the city by midday, giving us enough time in the afternoon to visit the beautiful Cathedral of San Salvador in the old part of town.

A few kilometers before reaching Oviedo, we were confronted outside a bar by a bunch of youths with shaven heads. "Franco! Franco! Viva Espania!" , they shouted trying to provoke us by throwing empty beer cans at us.

"Avoid the energy. Don't go into their space," Chuck whispered. "Just keep on walking."

Out of the corner of my eye, I noticed the wide-eyed bar owner ducking behind the counter.

A hate-filled almost demonic fanatic face with bloodshot eyes, broken teeth and clenched fists came up close to my face.

Suddenly I heard a screeching voice behind me. "Qué vergüenza!" – what a disgrace!

A matronly woman with gray hair and dressed in

black confronted the youths head-on. Her arms folded in front of her chest, and telling them off with a fiery burst of words. As if on command a group of farmers armed with pitchforks emerged from the shadows.

The extremists made a quick about-face, heading for their scooters as quick as their drunken legs could carry them.

"Los siento por eso" – sorry for that. "Buen Camino!" the woman said, leading us gently forward and pointing to a waymark showing the route to Oviedo.

CHAPTER THIRTEEN — CAMINO PRIMITIVO

For centuries, pilgrims on the Camino Primitivo have made a stop in Oviedo to pay homage to the "other shroud of Christ." Along with the Shroud of Turin, it is said to have been part of the cloth in which the body of Jesus was wrapped after being taken from the cross.

Known as the Sudarium (face cloth) or the "Cloth of Oviedo," it is said to have found its way to Spain from Palestine with Christians fleeing the Arab invasion of the Iberian Peninsula. King Alfonso II, who turned back the Arab invasion, established his court in Oviedo, and brought the relic to the city.

The king built a chapel with a holy chamber in 840 to shelter the cloth and other relics, around which the Cathedral of San Salvador was built and reconstructed over the centuries.

Early medieval pilgrim writings even argued that pilgrims who had paid homage to St. James in Santiago but not visited the holy chamber of the Cathedral in Oviedo had visited the servant and neglected the master.

Whether there is a link between the Sudarium and the

Shroud of Turin remains speculation and the object of continued scientific research. What has been established is that the Sudarium was probably placed on the face of a man who had been beaten on the front and back of the head, leaving stains of AB blood on the shroud.

Days were needed to explore the cathedral. After a day wandering through the streets and enjoying the lively atmosphere in the city, I was exhausted.

The contrast of walking most of the day in nature and then being confronted by the blaring noise of a Spanish city with the television in every café seemingly on full volume was difficult to bear. The senses of hearing and smell become fine-tuned in the countryside and man-made noise seemed like a violation.

Early that evening we took time to meditate in the cathedral, its walls so thick that almost all the noise of the city was drowned out. The images and statues of Jesus, Mary and the Apostles were so awe-inspiring that they almost come alive when you look closely at the details.

There was Jesus holding his open heart, as if telling the observer: Go into your heart mind.

The central Gothic altarpiece, depicting numerous scenes from the life of Christ, was a work of master artists.

I made a commitment to meditate and observe more closely every chapel and work of art on the next stages of the Camino. In the tradition of the many pilgrims that had gone before I would leave a marker stone for all those of my ancestors, going down three generations and past and future relationships, and for the people who had been of major influence in my life.

Chuck had recommended the ritual soon after our first meeting, but I was not far enough down the road at the time to truly fathom what it would do for my personal transformation.

It was a warm night so I kept the hotel window open, only to be woken in the middle of the night by angry shouting between what sounded like a mother and daughter having a "minor" disagreement, plates crashing to the floor in the process.

The hotel manager yanked open a window and bellowed into the courtyard, which immediately put a stop to the noise.

I had difficulty falling asleep again, my mind wandering back to my past life and wondering what my future would be like after the Camino.

The path had a subtle way of making you aware that the wheel of life was change and evolution. Moving forward out of the comfort zone was following the soul path, the road to new experience and opening the door to a new perspective.

What we believe to be a comfort zone is a veil of obsession that keeps us in a very uncomfortable zone of frustration, the low level of toxic emotions, stagnation and failure. The even tide of stability is an illusion. For a while we feel that the whole universe is aligned in favor of us, only to have it all fall apart at a moment's notice.

Once you are on the path you have no choice: You

just keep going. While walking you realize that the failures and ups-and-downs are part of the lesson of letting go of attachments, and that you have to be prepared for a realignment with changing circumstances.

Conformism is the low average of the masses who complain and make everyone but themselves responsible for their misery: the bad childhood, the employer, the government, the husband or wife, the children or whoever else comes to mind. It's always someone else. There is always a reason why something cannot be done or why an issue cannot be addressed. Life just dealt them a bad hand of cards.

As Santiago comes ever closer, it pulls like a giant magnet of life, ever faster to the final destination. And afterward, a higher goal, a next cycle, a new dimension?

You meet wonderful fellow pilgrims, hear their stories and how they grappled with their "bad hand of cards," suffered in the darkness of a pit, then realign themselves, overcome the obstacles and emerged all the stronger and wiser.

Friendships develop and grow within a short space of time. And then you say goodbye. You meet some people again on the way, and others, with whom you have shared intimate details of your life, you never see again. You forget to ask them for their name, telephone number or e-mail address.

What remains of significance is that you met them at the right moment to hear a message, to mull over a question or to change your own perspective.

As Chuck would say so: "There are problems, dude

and there are difficulties, dude and most of the time we are just dealing with the difficulties."

We were both at a point of our pilgrimage where we needed a day to chill out. It was also a good feeling to wake up in the morning knowing there would be at least another hour to sleep and nobody was in the next bunk bed to disturb you.

As Chuck put it: "The Camino is not a crucifixion. It's about learning to look after yourself, to be compassionate to yourself. Only if you are mindful of yourself will you be mindful of your surroundings and of others.

"And by the way, dude. It's all in the scriptures, in Mark where a scribe asks Jesus about what commandment is the most important, to which he replies:

The most important: Hear O Israel: The Lord our God is one Lord, and you shall love the Lord your God with all your heart and with all your soul and with all your mind and with all your strength. The second is this: Love your neighbor as yourself. No other commandment is greater than these."

There was a deeper meaning behind the carvings, paintings and statues in the churches and cathedrals, illustrating the love for the inner Christ, the inner child: The Madonna's caring gaze on the child in her arms, the protective arms of St. James and St. Francis holding the baby Jesus.

It could not be that God, the universe or creation wanted us to suffer or to be unhappy and very often it was a personal choice or action that led to suffering.

The image came to mind of pilgrims bearing a heavy cross on their shoulders and whipping themselves like the radical monks of medieval times.

Many a modern pilgrim too, has ignored bleeding feet and swollen knees, forcing her or himself to go on, despite a body rebelling against every step. There was something masochistic about it.

"It is surprising considering that there are no real rules on how to do the Camino," I commented.

"Of course, everyone has and should have a different pace," Chuck responded.

"Some pilgrims do the Camino in stages over several years during vacation time, others during a sabbatical or after retirement."

I had noticed several types of pilgrims on the Camino.

There was the traditional peregrino, walking the entire Camino on foot with a backpack, sleeping overnight in a bunk bed in an Albergue hostel. Then there were the bicygrinos, those guys who see the Camino as some type of physical adventure and try to reach the next stage as fast as possible on their mountain bike.

Getting ever more popular were the "donkey-grinos" doing the Camino with a donkey in tow. They had a problem when the donkey decided to call it a day, and obstinately refused to move, despite much pleading, cajoling and angry mutterings.

The tourgrinos, were day trippers, who poured out of

air conditioned buses to walk short sections of the path, to be picked up again for lunch at the next luxury hotel.

"You shouldn't be so judgmental about it, dude," Chuck laughed. "The Camino has been an income generator for those towns along the path for generations – for the church dioceses, for the innkeepers, the taxi drivers, the restaurant owners and the cleaner women.

"The ancient guide-books on the Camino are full of stories of the nobility, popes, kings and queens doing the Camino with an entire entourage of carriages, horses and servants.

"Only the mode of transport and fashion have changed somewhat, I guess," Chuck said smiling as a group of cyclists whizzed past.

We were sitting in a café, having a café con leche. At the table next to us a group of teenage girls were busy on their smart-phones. It was ironic that the social media connected people from widely separated places better than ever before, but disconnected people from those right next to them.

On TV a journalist was interviewing a group of teenagers on the latest gaming fad – Pokémon.

"The power of distraction at work," Chuck commented, and I was reminded of my own life back home its rhythm of checking and answering e-mails and falling asleep in front of the TV after work.

"So often I find myself looking for something on the Internet and then being distracted by something else that pops up. You end up occupying yourself for hours with unimportant stuff," I said.

"Well, the objective of mass media is to reach as many people as possible. The idea is to pull you away from something you are doing. We have enormous forces at work here, and it's very difficult to extract yourself once you have been entangled and are being pulled in a certain direction.

"Worst of all, you have to look at the information you are being bombarded with from all directions 24-7. In most cases its toxic. It's bad news: catastrophes, the rich and famous misbehaving, bad traits such as narcissism and greed being propounded as virtues.

"I'm sorry for sounding all preachy again, dude, " Chuck said with a chuckle.

"Every generation has its challenges. And the biggest challenge we face is to discern the truth, your inner truth and soul's purpose behind the smokescreen of distraction that the mass media throws at us from every direction.

"Character is determined by habits, and your habits determine how you live your life.

"So the question I'm asking you, and which we should all be asking ourselves, is: "Where is my focus? Where is, my attention going?

"Am I being pulled in this or that direction at whim and following the next latest message on mass media? Or do I train myself with positive habits that align me with an awakened state of consciousness?"

"I can't stand this happy culture, especially coming from all those best seller titles, coming from your side of the pond," I commented.

"Then you're getting me wrong, dude," Chuck argued.

"We know from our walk on the Camino that we often can't choose with what we are confronted with. We hope for a nice sunny day and are drenched with rain. We hope to meet nice people and are insulted by right-wing radicals.

"We have high and low moments. That's life. It's the yin and yang. If you think you have to be on a high all the time, you are building an illusion.

"There is an old saying attributed to a Persian ruler, who asked his sages for one quote applicable at all times and in all situations. After long deliberation,, they came up with:

'This too, shall pass.'

"The challenge is how fast you can get out of those low moments, to realign, to get back onto that higher plateau and not to be pulled into the maelstrom that feeds on toxic emotions such as fear and anger.

"Strengthening your character with positive habits such as gratefulness, love, compassion and generosity is what it's all about. It's the core message of all the major teachings – think about it."

Chuck took another long sip from his almost cold café con leche.

"Let's hit the road," I said.

"All for it, dude. Let's go."

The way forward is the way that carries you into the future. Around every bend lies unknown territory.

Ancient masters sent their students on a journey to uncharted places, for it is within the unknown that the walk starts from within. And from self-recognition comes compassion.

It was a lonely walk to Escamplero through the towns of Loriana, Fabarin and Gallegos along a winding path of luscious green valleys.

A nation closes down for siesta, with dogs chained behind high fencing announcing our presence with angry barking.

Alone, and with Chuck far ahead of me, I learned my personal mantra:

I am centered.

I am aligned with my heart and soul center.

I fully accept my inner self.

I fully accept myself in the here and now.

I inhale acceptance and exhale gratitude.

I am connected to my soul path and in service to higher evolution.

I am a disciple of everlasting light.

To find the path it was necessary to become the path.

The Camino Primitivo was the most challenging, and at the same time, one the most beautiful sections of the

Camino.

It would take us about two weeks of easy walking to get to Santiago from Oviedo.

There were obstacles to be overcome, wandering thoughts that disturbed the spirit.

It was a challenge to remain in the light with positive thoughts and avoid being pulled away by the rubbish of a mind occupied with what it no longer needed.

Are the thoughts predominantly negative or predominantly positive?

"Where the thoughts go, the energy flows," Chuck said in one of our discussions.

I soon realized that one of the hardest things was to train the mind to remain focused. It was like a butterfly attracted to a hundred flowers at once.

So often on the Camino I had to learn the lesson that when my mind was distracted, I would inevitably miss the yellow way-mark and get lost.

Chuck was waiting for me at our agreed meeting point at the Albergue in Escamplero. The only restaurant in town was closed for the day, so that we decided to cook dinner from what was available in a little shop.

We were soon joined by a group of fellow peregrinos: Ana, a Danish student; Kristine, a German teacher, and Ronaldo, an Italian engineer.

Ronaldo insisted on preparing the pasta while the rest of us helped with the salad. Ana made a traditional

Danish berry dessert, a tongue twister called Rødgrød med fløde.

We all had a go at pronouncing. Out came butchered words such as "red mat flat" or "rod met fatty". Ronaldo had a particularly inventive version: "watko ma fleto". We all had a lot of fun that evening, laughing at our try at foreign words.

After our second glass of wine the topics turned to more serious issues from climate change to bull fighting.

"So you say we have to focus our mind on the positive? I can't do that if I see that so much has to be done to make our world a better place," Ana said, looking at Chuck.

"You get me wrong," Chuck replied. "It's not about burying your head in the sand and ignoring the problems in the world. I admire people like you who have the courage to organize protest against political leaders.

"My gripe is with the dosage. We are being brainwashed with negativity."

"But that is just the way the world is," Ana said.

"I disagree," Chuck said. "Part of the world is like that. How many good things are happening, changing, evolving in a positive way that we never hear about.

"It's the law of resonance. Negativity breeds negativity and positivity triggers positivity. Where your attention goes, the energy goes."

"I don't quite get you," Ana countered. "Some things just make me angry, like seeing those poor dogs tied to chains and kept in cages. Why do they keep dogs as pets if they can't look after them?

"Even the donkeys and horses are tied to poles in the meadows."

Kristine, who had been listening closely all the while, summed up her feelings: "I see a common thread here. Fighting bulls, chasing bulls through streets, it's like the animals are objects and not living beings. It's like there is fear of the animal side of human nature inside that has to be locked away and tied up."

"That is why I prefer Buddhism to Christianity," Ana said. "At least that is one religion that places all living beings on the same level."

Ronaldo had his take on it: "It's different in the cities. But out here in the country, people see dogs and cats not as pets but as farm animals like every other animal. Dogs are guarding property, protecting sheep from wolves or accompanying hunters. Cats are for catching mice. And as for bulls. This has been part of Spanish culture for centuries. It has nothing to do with religion."

The discussion went on for a while, Ronaldo soon excusing himself. Asking a peregrino why he was walking the Camino was a question I was beginning to find too intrusive.

Just by talking and confiding in each other, we made the question irrelevant and sometimes the motive for walking changed on the path.

Ronaldo was one of the peregrinos who was"walking things off" by going at a pace most others could not keep up with, avoiding all conversation out on the path as the emotional clutter gradually released itself, opening up space for new experience.

And it was that space, as Chuck said "that can then be nourished with inner peace, forgiveness and compassion. You in fact are working on becoming a better human being."

CHAPTER FOURTEEN — A PATH LESS TRAVELED

It was my 30th day on the Camino on the morning I left Escamplero. It would take another two weeks of walking to get to Santiago. It was time for a little review.

Walking the Camino had been so much more than a mere physical exercise. It was becoming more and more obvious to me that the special people you meet on the Camino and the long history of this ancient path had its own magic in changing old systems of thought and belief.

I had started out on the path, stumbling along aimlessly and was close to giving up when Chuck came along, opening up his tool box of wisdom. And there were so many others from whom I was learning. There were problems and difficulties in life, and mostly we were preoccupied with difficulties.

One of the difficulties that could easily be prevented was cracked feet and blisters.

Rubbing the feet with a cream made from deer fat made them soft and supple. The problem of wet boots was also easily solved: Chuck's recipe was to waterproof the boots with a candle and to soften the leather with a hair dryer.

Removing emotional clutter was much harder but in a different way made walking that much easier, especially when you start the day with a positive attitude:

I am grateful for the gift of life.

I am grateful that I can walk this path

I am grateful for all the great teachers in my life

And I was beginning to learn to flip the switch. Releasing toxic emotional clutter right at the start of the day would inevitably set a positive note for the rest of it.

A Camino lesson was that happiness is a state of mind. Emotions, feelings and perceptions – be they of a negative or a positive nature – came and went like a passing cloud in a blue sky.

On the lonely, less traveled Camino Primitivo, there was more time for that look deep inside.

How much was I blocked and hindered by emotional obstacles from the past and from what I had inherited from the generations that went before!

There was a need to forgive family members for the feuds over last wills and testaments, and for the pain inflicted by casual remarks that remained frozen in the sub-conscious. There were the deep scars from separations and divorces that needed healing.

Chuck had explained that in the Middle Ages, families came together to sponsor one member of the clan to walk the Camino and heal what needed to be

healed in the family by obtaining the blessing of St.
James in Santiago.

Very often these pilgrims paid the ultimate sacrifice,
many an old stone cross along the path reminding us that
walking the Camino in those days was an enormous
challenge as disease, robbery and physical exhaustion
took their toll.

"The Western mind has lost its way by losing the
connection to ancestral roots," Chuck had said to me in
one of our conversations.

"Respect for ancestral elders guiding one's soul path
from a different dimension is deeply embedded in all
ancient cultures. What gives us the arrogance to think
that we know it all and can do it all alone?" he asked.

But I was learning. The Camino Primitivo was a start.
I left a pebble on the first marker stone outside
Escamplero, near a beautiful old chapel, for the
generation on my father's side forced to flee France in
the late 16th century after it launched a violent war of
persecution against the Protestant Huguenot movement
that culminated in the St. Bartholomew's Day massacre
in 1572.

Many of the wealthy and prominent Huguenot
aristocrats of the day had gathered in Paris for the
wedding of the Protestant Henry III of Navarre, the
future Henry IV of France. Five days after the wedding,
riots erupted with Catholic mobs going on a killing spree
on the eve of the feast of Bartholomew the Apostle
during the night of August 23-24.

The killing spread throughout Paris and the rural areas

of France, forcing many Huguenot families to flee to England, the Netherlands and Germany.

The information was sparse and I had learned most of the family history as a child from Grandma. The experience, however, seemed to have embedded in our family genes a deep resentment of Catholicism and a rigid and dogmatic Protestant belief system.

Several of the sons in ensuing generations chose to be Protestant pastors or missionaries, my grandfather being the last in the line of steadfast theologians well versed in all Bible matters and the intricate differences between Protestants and Catholics, such as not sharing Holy Communion.

Catholics and Protestants certainly didn't marry each other, in Grandpa's world, so you can imagine his consternation and anger when my father fell in love and married a Catholic, my mother.

"You don't have my blessing for this marriage!" were his words when Dad told him that he was going to marry "this Catholic woman."

"Your father might be speaking for himself, but you do have my blessing," was Grandma's response. Behind her soft-spoken gentleness was a lady who stood her ground. She was far more capable of discerning the character of a person behind the veil of religion, nationality or color. And she had made up her mind that Mother was going to be a perfectly suitable wife for her son.

The deep prejudice between my Catholic grandparents and the Protestant side of the family, however, left a deep mark on the family, especially when it came to what religion us kids were to be raised in. Dad promptly decided to become the first agnostic in the family while Mother remained a devout, although seldom church-going Catholic, until she died from cancer at the early age of 48, never fully recovering from the hurt she had suffered from her side of the family for marrying a Protestant.

By the time, I was a teenager, I was rebelliously rejecting all things religion, having felt its ugly dogmatic sting from an early age.

So, in some dimension of my ancestral past there was a voice that called me to go on a very traditional Catholic pilgrimage route, if for nothing else, than to heal an ancestral wound.

The path from Escamplero to the town of Grado was a relatively easy 17-kilometer (10.5 miles) walk. But from the town of Grado it was a steep climb that soon offered a beautiful view of the town and its surroundings.

I had agreed to meet Chuck in the monastery of San Salvador in the town of Cornellana.

Its history is well documented. It was founded in 1024 by Infanta Cristina, daughter of King Bermudo II and Queen Velasquita, who retired to this convent after the death of her husband, Ordoño. It was passed to the monks of Cluny in 1122 so that they could establish a Benedictine monastery, and since the Middle Ages has had a history of catering to St. James pilgrims.

Over the doorway leaving the monastery vegetable garden, there is a relief of a bear nursing a girl, with two lion heads on either side. According to legend, Infanta Cristina got lost in the Asturian woods as a child and survived after being protected by a bear.

Part of the monastery includes a Romanesque church rebuilt in the 17th century with a vaulted ceiling and the addition of a high choir at the west end.

For decades it was desolate, parts of it being used as a butter factory, until it was declared a national monument in 1931. Massive renovations, starting with the repair of the roof giving a good indication of the former glory of the complex.

A wing of the monastery has been converted into a comfortable Albergue hostel and I found Chuck in the courtyard cleaning his boots.

"Good job, dude. I've been waiting to have a beer with you at the café down the road."

Over a cold beer and a meal consisting of traditional Asturian soup followed by French fries and chicken breast, Chuck told me it was not unusual for karmic issues going back generations to surface during a walk on the Camino.

"We tend to laugh it off when we hear a preacher telling off his congregation to be wary of Satan. The battle between the dark and the light forces is at a crucial point in history because Satan has become more devious in his disguises. The battle lines are not that clearly visible and we tend to look outside, not realizing that the battle within only expresses itself in what is expressed on the outside. You have to be wary, very wary."

I did not realize at the time how clear a warning Chuck was giving me that afternoon. He probably sensed the danger that lay ahead.

We spent a long time discussing the differences between raised awareness and lower consciousness. Humanity apparently goes through long cycles of both at turning points in history.

Raised awareness was the striving for the common good, service to humanity and the cultivation of values such as compassion, humility, love and forgiveness.

Lower consciousness was ego-driven and triggered by toxic emotions such as fear, greed, hate, anger and narcissism. As Chuck so emphatically put it: "It's a 'me first' and fuck everyone else attitude. You see it on an individual level and on a national level."

Later at the Albergue hostel, Kristine the German girl was worried about our Polish friend, Andrzej. His feet looked bad so Kristine went to a pharmacy to get him special sticking tape to dress the blisters on his toes and ankles. Apart from that, his knees were badly swollen.

We suggested to Andrzej that it might be wise to spend a day resting at the monastery. As if guessing our thoughts, he vehemently shook his head: "Santiago! Santiago!"

My dreams were haunted by images of peasants armed with pitch forks chasing people down dark avenues in the streets of Paris. Their eyes were bloodshot with hate and anger, spittle running from their mouths, which twisted into an ugly grimace each time they thrust a pitch fork into the body of another victim.

Then I, too, found myself running from a wild mob. The walls closed in on me until there was no room to escape. My back was against a wall. I woke up with a start. Someone was shaking me. It was Kristine.

"I'm sorry to wake you," she said "I'm really afraid. There is this guy across from my bed who keeps staring at me."

"Oh, no!," I moaned. It was the hobbit. He stared at me with an ugly grimace like one of those madmen who had chased me in my dream. And he was counting again: "one, two, three."

We moved Kristine's sleeping bag to the bunk bed next to mine, where she felt more comfortable. And she felt more at ease when I suggested that we walk together early the next morning.

CHAPTER FIFTEEN — DEMONS

Clouds were still hanging low as we climbed the hill. The sky opened momentarily, offering a fantastic view of the monastery of San Salvador and the town of Cornellana..

"You guys go ahead," Kristine panted. "I'm fine and sorry for the discomfort last night. I guess I was just a little overanxious regarding the hobbit."

It was early enough to walk off the shadows of the night. I needed time to reflect on family matters. Over generations, the family line had exchanged the dogma of Catholicism for the dogma of its own version of Protestantism.

Family members who went out of line with the generational pact were sidelined and ostracized. Others felt an obligation to continue the pact by going into the ministry, although I was not so sure about my grandfather, whose bitterness at not having pursued a well-paid career as an engineer surfaced on many an occasion.

Why couldn't humanity leave things alone and allow freedom for individual interpretation of scripture and soul path? From what I had learned on about the religious ceremonies in the monasteries on the path there was a time when doctrine and papal interpretation of scripture played a subordinate role.

Divine inspiration and insight were gained in meditative prayer, chanting liturgy, singing hymns, contemplating works of art and making a pilgrimage. Maybe humanity was turning full circle.

That morning I felt a lump in my throat. The backpack load seemed heavier than usual. The dreams of the previous night were still vividly present. The madly screaming crowd:

"Demon! Demon, confess!" they screamed with hate-filled eyes as I was marched in a procession through a medieval town, barefooted, shirtless and with a rope tied around my neck. The executioner, walking behind me, prodded me with a stick toward the center of the village, where a spot had been prepared for the execution.

They tied me tightly to a stake with ropes and chains, then piled layers of straw and wood around it. The smell of burning flesh. Excruciating pain in the feet, the knees the whole body. Bells tolling incessantly. Then nothing. Silence. No more pain. No more screaming, just silence.

Was this the surfacing of some karmic memory of a previous life? Was this the reason I had been afraid all my life of larger crowds, the reason for my nervousness when having to speak in public. I recalled myself in a school class, stuttering through a summary of any essay, facing the derision of the class, the angry look from the teacher, feeling the lump in my throat, the sweat of fear in clammy hands and feet.

I was relieved to find Andrzej at the top of the hill. He was lying in the shade of an oak tree. The guy was amazing, having left much earlier than all of us to keep his own pace, walking slowly, each step a step through pain. Yet his mood remained upbeat and cheerful.

"Dzien dobry! Buen Camino!" he beamed.

Despite not being able to speak each others languages, meeting a fellow peregrino at that moment was a welcome relief. We didn't have to converse in a language that we both understood to have a heart-to-heart connection. Andrzej was one of those rare individuals whose aura through their mere presence created a positive atmosphere.

We shared an apple while I told him about my dream. He said something in Polish, giving me a gentle, comforting pat on the back. It was a small gesture with a big effect.

My walk seemed easier, and the clouded and somber mood of that morning simply dissipated like the fog that lifted soon afterwards as sunlight finally penetrated the gray skies.

Overly confident, I missed an important waymark, suddenly finding myself in the ruins of a deserted group of old stone farmhouses. It would take me longer to walk back as I knew roughly the direction to the town of Salas.

I kept walking along the path until I heard steps behind me. Glancing backward I saw a stooped figure walking behind me. I felt chills run down my spine as I looked into those dark, expressionless eyes, that twisted nose, hardlower jaw. A demon?

When I increased my walking pace, the figure behind me did likewise. It got more frightening when the path narrowed, with rock walls on either side.

Suddenly a big black dog stood before me, blocking my path, baring its teeth and growling angrily. I was trapped.

Behind me I heard a guttural laughter of derision. Turning around, I could see no sign of the demon. He seemed to have disappeared, but where? There were rock walls on both sides. I stood my ground before the snarling dog. Another demon?

With all the energy left in me, I clambered up one of the rock walls, the dog snapping at my feet, and dropped myself on the other end. The guttural laughter followed me.

I scrambled into the undergrowth, thorn bushes tearing at my legs. I ran, stumbled, fell, and got up again.

Then I stopped to catch my breath, silence, except for my heavy panting and the sound of my heart beating against my chest. The shrill cry of a blackbird cut through the air. Had I imagined all of this? Was I going mad? Had my mind started playing tricks on me?

Once again I was lost and had to find my sense of direction. This was a moment when I needed protection. "Just lead me, just lead me," I pleaded, finally finding an overgrown forest path.

Positioned on a rocky ledge was a carved Madonna, her gentle, carved features blurred by a mossy film, yet looking almost uncannily alive.

Here was the Great Mother, offering her protection. Above me, below me, to the left of me, to the right of me, before me and behind me. Amen!

A glowing feeling of warmth and the love of the goddess enveloped my body as I felt at one with what had been in my life and what would come on a higher plane of consciousness.

After the frightening experience of separation and loss came the recognition that the experiences of the past were beginning to shape a new future.

Much later I heard the sound of a rushing stream, the spring water helping to soothe the pain from the thorns in my legs. Washing my face helped to clear my mind.

Finally, there was the river, and the sound of motor vehicles on the road that led to Salas.

I found Chuck, Kristine and Andrzej outside a cafe near the old church, having a café con leche, all of them expressing great surprise at my being so late.

"I got lost," I admitted, still contemplating whether to share my story of the demon.

"You got more than lost," Chuck said, analyzing my state of mind.

I told them what had happened, sharing my unease about the demon or whether I had just imagined it all.

"No, you didn't," Kristine blurted out.

"I saw him, too. I was further behind you and he came at me from behind a tree, snarling like a dog. I shouted at him to go away and he just laughed. Fortunately, at that point Andrzej came around the corner and the demon just seemed to disappear into thin air."

"This is not so unusual," Chuck said. "We tend to scoff at people who tell us these stories. But demons and the devil are real. It's part of their camouflage to make us believe they are not real.

"Where there is much light, like on the Camino, there is also shadow. Light and shadow co-exist. We cannot see the good in comparison to the bad or happiness in comparison to unhappiness.

"It's all actually a good sign. The demons show themselves where there is fear, and it is good to have fear sometimes. It's a survival instinct. It gives us the energy to redirect and to refocus."

I realized that the demon had in fact pushed me to the path that led me to the Madonna, engaging in a real spiritual experience.

CHAPTER SIXTEEN — LA ESPINA

We walked into the town of La Espina as thick fog descended, making us acutely aware that this was mountain country where the weather could change in an instant.

It was an almost mystical atmosphere, with shutters down, and only a single donkey cart moving down the road on this siesta afternoon. The first Albergue hostel in town was closed.

"The other one in town is open," said a stocky man who reminded me of Baloo the bear character in 'The Jungle Book.' His name was Esteban and he was walking the Camino with his donkey, Willy and his black mongrel dog, Moro. They had been on the various paths of the Camino for the past three years.

Judging from his unkept appearance and dirty clothing, I gathered that he had been sleeping outside with his animals. From a conversation, he had with Chuck, we later found out that he had been a building contractor in southern Spain before his company went bankrupt. Having lost everything, and after a troublesome divorce, he now chose to live a "stress-free, minimalistic life on the Camino."

Esteban spent the cold winter months on a farm near Santiago, where he helped out as a handyman in exchange for lodging and food.

A friendly lady in the grocery store gave us the key to the Albergue hostel. We offered to pay for Esteban's stay overnight but he kindly refused, saying it was not raining and that he wanted to spend the night with Willy and Moro underneath a tree in the park.

The Albergue hostel had a modern washing machine and dryer, so we were pretty fast in completing our daily routine of cleaning socks, underwear and other clothing for the next day.

We were getting a little concerned about Andrzej, when he finally arrived a good three hours later, limping badly. The ever-friendly lady from the grocery store explained to him in sign language and with an excited flurry of words that it would be no problem for him to stay another night and get a good rest.

"No, No. Camino Santiago!" he replied, his sunburned face getting redder. A good meal with a red wine and an extra night's rest was all he needed.

Andrzej, Kristine, Chuck and I were the only peregrinos at the Albergue that night. We decided to cook a Camino dinner together and enjoy a few good bottles of Rioja wine.

The fog outside had gotten so intense that we could barely see the buildings across the street when we looked out the window.

"I feel guilty leaving Esteban out there while we are here in the cozy Albergue," Kristine said.

"Very often it's easier to give a gift than to accept a gift," Chuck said. "He will have his reasons."

"I think it's pretty hard living like that," she said. "I really feel sorry for him. He must have gone through a lot of pain to make a decision like that."

"Well he doesn't appear to be all that unhappy with the choice he has made," I said. "Better living on the Camino than living in a homeless shelter."

"I think that's cynical," Kristine said.

"Where we are is a result of the choices we have made," Chuck said.

"Taking responsibility for the consequences of all our actions is the first step to self-awareness and enlightenment."

"But what about the external events that we don't have under control, like a recession, political turmoil or a natural disaster?" I asked.

"Of course, we don't have that under control," Chuck added. "But what we do have under control is how we react to those disasters and setbacks in life, and how fast we can realign and kick-start ourselves to a new beginning. That is indeed a choice.

"I could sit back and say that it was my former wife's decision to leave me at a point in life when I really needed her. But now if I think back about it. I was just as responsible for the breakdown of our marriage. I was in denial about the many signs of a dysfunctional relationship and didn't act. I didn't do my part in telling her every day that I appreciated and loved her. I took our relationship for granted and pursued so many other things that my wife started feeling neglected and not seen or heard."

"Why are you men all like that!" Kristine said angrily. "You all seem to go into a state of non-response in the course of a relationship. Every one of my girlfriends I talk to has the same problem. That's why I'm single and I'm happy to be that way."

"And you women are all emotion, that is misdirected and filled with over expectation," I said.

Chuck listened a while in silence as we related the wounds of the relationships of the past. Taking a slow sip from his glass of wine, he mused.

"Hmm, the pain is an expression of the duality within us that seeks completion. The delusion is that as we go on the soul search of merging the opposites within us, we seek that self-unification in the love of a man or a woman. For a while it works as we fall into romantic love, raising our beloved onto an unrealistic pedestal.

"We banish thoughts that the person we have fallen in love with also has issues to deal with like we all have. As romantic love fades and the reality of life sets in, the sexual attraction levels off, and we become disappointed and angry at the person we fell in love with.

"Our partner has failed in not filling that void within

us, that self-unification that is still trying to manifest itself.

"The secret is that you have to start loving yourself, the goddess within you, unconditionally. And it is an ongoing process with starts and stops and disappointments along the way."

Chuck looked at me long and hard. "Your meeting with the goddess in the woods is a very important first step into non-dualism. It marks the beginning. Enlightenment is not a one-off, wham-bang-thing, and then complete, dude. It evolves and grows, all the time, dude."

What we call God is growth and evolution of life in all its amazing forms and facets. We are all on a journey to spiritual completion, and when a cycle is completed, a new door opens to a new world of consciousness and discovery.

We meet souls on our path who trigger something and then leave us to work it out alone. Chuck described it as the contractual agreement that souls make with each other before they are born.

CHAPTER SEVENTEEN — HEALING RELATIONSHIPS

Walking was becoming so much easier. After the first aching steps in the morning, it was as if my body switched to autopilot, carrying me along the rolling green hills like an eagle in the sky locking into a thermal glide.

It was exhilarating to smell the fresh morning air, feel the moisture of dew on my face and to watch rainbow-colored glitter in spider webs in the dawn sunlight.

This feeling of being alive was new and at the same time old, harking back to the days of childhood with the joyful climbing of trees, swimming in rivers and rolling in freshly cut grass.

Along an ancient cobblestone path, near Tineo, I met up again with Esteban, his donkey, Willy and dog, Moro who ran ahead, scouting the territory.

As we rounded a corner, Willy spotted a group of horses running towards us. Craning his neck, he stopped dead in his tracks and let out an ear-piercing "eeyore!

Eeyore!"

Esteban plopped to the ground. "Have to wait..."

But then he knew the art of motivating a donkey and began rummaging in his bag. He pulled out a carrot and lured Willy along with it until the horses were out of sight. Walking the Camino with a donkey was a particular challenge. A person like me, though walking it for the first time had to deal with the daily challenges of the mind.

By now I was physically fit enough to easily walk 25 to 27 kilometers (15.5 to 16.7 miles) a day, but the challenges of the mind were getting tougher by the day. The path was not letting me take a break.

The first part of walking the Camino was the path of crucifixion: enduring the physical pain of hurting feet and legs, the thirst, the heat, and overcoming the urge to simply throw in the towel.

And, as I learned from talking to pilgrims along the way the physical challenge alone was too much. On the other hand, it was amazing to see people like Greta, who ignored all medical advice and just kept walking and growing spiritually.

My confrontation with inner and outer demons was my path of death. I knew I had to let go of so many of the old demons that still haunted my life. The conversation of the previous night had made me all too aware of my own shattered relationships.

And that was the point. Life was all about relationships, maintaining and nurturing friendships, family ties, and keeping up communication with the people who really mattered. So often had I missed the point by focusing all my attention on career and external issues and values that now seemed so irrelevant.

"You switch off and lock yourself into your own world. I feel very alone and invisible to you. I need to leave you for my own well-being."

Marla was very direct in expressing her needs in a relationship, and I was unable to give her what she wanted. We had met on a blind date arranged by a friend. I remembered how I fell in love with this beautiful woman with a self-deprecating humor and sophisticated bearing. After our third date, she pulled me into her bedroom and we had wild sex for the rest of the night.

But we lived in different cities and neither of us were willing to give up our independence. Our weekends were packed with activities as if that could make up for the hollowness that started creeping into the relationship like a festering sore. She wanted a family and children. I didn't. The arguments started increasing.

The frustrations and disappointments found expression in those long moments of silence when we had nothing more to say to each other, let alone have sex.

As a good friend confided to me over a beer: "If the sex no longer works, it's over, my friend."

After a weekend, spent fighting and arguing over little things, Marla picked up a plate and threw it to the ground so that it shattered into a thousand pieces. "That's it, that's our relationship. It's over."

After nearly eight years together, we never saw each other again after that weekend. A friend of a friend heard that she had moved to Australia after meeting a rich businessman on one of her public relations assignments.

But the ghost of Marla that haunted me that day was telling me I had not really dealt with the hurt and the lessons to be learned from that relationship and those that followed.

After Marla, I was incapable of opening my heart and emotions to another woman. The hurt and fear of being hurt again were too deep.

Before entering the town of Tineo, I passed a sculpture of a peregrino standing on a sun-dial in the shape of a scallop. He was facing the path and looking away from Tineo, so I took that as a message to continue walking to Campiello that day.

But I needed a café con leche, feeling sad and a lump in my throat. And what happens at such moments on the Camino. You find a fellow Peregrino who lifts your spirits and tells you the world is not such a bad place after all.

Andrzej and Kristine were having a beer on the square in the middle of the town, cheerfully calling me over.

While Andrzej simply accepted in silence our conversation in English, which he didn't understand, I told Kristine about my pain from Marla.

"If something is not healed, it will come again and again to haunt you, Jake. You must forgive her and yourself," she said.

And at the next way mark, as we were going up the hill out of Tineo, Kristine taught me a prayer for which I will forever be thankful to her.

"Jake, I wish you a good life with all my heart. May you be liberated from the toxic forces of anger and hate. May you be liberated from the sadness about what has changed and no longer exists. May you be liberated from the pain of body, mind and spirit. May you have a good life that takes you into higher and higher realms."

Then she asked me to repeat the same prayer for Marla. It took me a while. "It's difficult," I said.

"Marla, I wish you with all my heart..." I had to stop. My voice was shaky and faltering. But Kristine insisted. "See if it really feels right for you and if you need more time."

I needed a few more minutes. And then I said the prayer. I imagined a different Marla. We had made a pact on a soul level to teach each other something during the time we were together. Now it was time to move on.

And there was more to follow that day. I met up again with Chuck at the Monastery of San Miguel de Barcena which requires a little detour from the path to Campiello.

The building, dating back to the 13th century, contains Romanesque architecture and a 16th century chapel located on the north side of the main complex.

We heard the chirping of a blackbird. We had been taken back to the Middle Ages.

"You are right in the middle of your path of death," Chuck said, carving a flat piece of wood.

There was a mixed feeling of relief and pain in my chest from the ritual I had performed that morning with Kristine at the waymark.

Marla represented all the painful relationships, unfinished business and traumas that still occupied my sub-consciousness.

"Take this and hang it around your neck," Chuck said, tying the piece of wood around my neck with a string so that it hung directly over my heart.

On the wood stood the words: "om mani padme hung" the Buddhist mantra for healing the heart.

"As a student once asked his teacher:

'Why do I say the mantra on my heart and not in my heart?'

"The Master paused and said; 'Because if it is on your heart, it starts working to open the heart. And when the heart is open with all its hurt and pain, then the healing can start."

I felt my body shaking uncontrollably. Tears were running down my cheeks. The pain in my chest was excruciating. Was I having a heart attack?

"You will be fine, dude," Chuck comforted me. "Just let it happen. Just let it be."

Unlike my nature, I gave him a big hug, thanking him profusely. He was such an important mentor on the path. Chuck looked at me intently.

"This is the point in time when I will be pulling back

a little. Devotion to a teacher can become the greatest obstacle to spiritual growth, and I am not a master. Those least followed are often the greatest masters, and the greatest master is the one within that needs to be awakened."

Clasping my mantra necklace close to my chest, with Chuck following behind, I continued my walk. I was beginning to understand.

For a large part of my life I had just gone through the motions: getting up in the morning, going to work, coming home. Somewhere along the line, I had lost my enthusiasm, my passion, my zeal – the will to follow and to listen to my heart.

It was the magic buried within that the Greeks called "theos," the God within.

Opening the heart and going through the pain was an essential part of self-recognition, self-acceptance and self-love. After that first big pain, I had closed my heart out of fear of experiencing that pain again, of falling back into that abyss.

Above the altar in one of the chapels I passed was an image of Jesus with his chest ripped open, revealing an open heart – wounded, bloodied, but alive.

I had always failed to see that suffering pain, the crucifixion and "death" of something we once had is what shook us into new perception, a new dimension of spiritual growth, and especially empathy and love, which makes us truly human.

But for generations this question has continued to

torment: 'How can God, the Christ, the embodiment of peace, love and compassion, allow evil and pain to happen?'

So often I had been deluded. When I thought, things were just going fine, and everything was good, life threw a curve ball that broke it all up.

I discussed at length with Chuck the issue. He mused a while, massaging his chin while thinking and looking at the sky as if seeking an answer from above.

"We tend to look at such issues too superficially, from an exterior perspective, as if God were both light and darkness. But this duality is really inside us and is our distorted picture of God. The issue of suffering is actually at the heart of the Christian story.

"Jesus blesses those who are suffering, who mourn and are persecuted. Why? It is when people are in pain and looking inward that they feel their higher self and soul path.

"He who is in pain is cleansed by it, finding, with the light, life and pain relieving love and compassion. Those who are in pain are actually closer to enlightenment than those who are deluding themselves that everything is just going fine and that they couldn't be happier.

"If we take that first step to avoid blaming everyone and everything outside us responsible for our pain, discover that by transforming self, the painful circumstances around us are also transformed.

"For those who remain obstinate and refuse to take the path of learning, the pain becomes all the more intense the longer they walk.

"It's actually so simple," Chuck laughed. "We just don't want to get it," he said, picking up a stone and throwing it into the woods. "If you don't work on yourself, fate takes over and pushes your head into the muddy water until you start getting it.

"It boils down to what the sages of old described as man's trinity of destiny:

"Recognize yourself! Be yourself and live your destiny. By wandering through the muddy water of the trinity comes the recognition of God.

"The more we perceive the sense of meaning and lesson to be learned the process of pain, the higher we walk on the plane of light.

"When we accept our pain with humility in quiet solitude, our eyes are opened to the relief of pain by discovering the God within. He who accepts suffering as a companion is on the path toward completing the outer cycle and entering the kingdom of peace, joy and fearlessness that comes from the eternal clarion call of 'fear not – I am with you!'

When I heard Chuck speaking like this, it was as if he were opening up some channel within, the tenor of his voice lower than normal, pausing, reflecting.

I made mental notes while listening to his words of wisdom as I still had such a long way to go. Here was a man who had done much of his soul-searching in deep pain. I was finally beginning to understand that there was more to just bearing one's cross through the daily burdens and challenges of life.

By resisting the burden of carrying the cross, you actually make your suffering worse. The medieval mystic Thomas of Kampen wrote: "If you bear your cross with an open heart, it will lead you."

Behind the dark shadow of suffering, the one on the path was already asking the question: "What is it that will wake me up, make me more mature and at one with my inner being and true God-nature?

This is how Chuck explained the breaking through of negative karma, getting out of the endless cycle of cause and effect and action followed by consequences.

I saw her image in front of me, clearly, as if in a lucid dream: the Mother Goddess holding her arms outstretched, the golden seam around her blue cloak illuminating so brightly that the image faded into the light as unexpectedly as it had appeared.

CHAPTER EIGHTEEN — MASTERY OF LOWER SELF

I had become aware of something deep inside that was profoundly sacred. What were just momentary, fleeting moments, had shaken me. The veil of illusion was lifting.

The sub conscious had one primary objective: striving towards enlightenment. Real humanness was deep inside, searching for the light of spirit, the God within.

But this was just the beginning of awakening on the spiritual path. There would be many more difficult paths of crucifixion, and deaths of the old ego would follow. It could take a lifetime or many more lifetimes.

I could fall back into the old life of the living dead or continue on this Path of mastering the shadow, the lower self and to move on to a higher frequency.

I was, to quote the poet Robert Frost, at a crossroads of two roads that diverged in a wood, and it was the one least traveled that made all the difference.

"There is no easy road, dude. You have to earn your

way to enlightenment by transforming the lower self and creating the bridge to your soul path," Chuck said as we sat drinking our café con leche in the town of Campiello at the end of our day's walk.

"It's like walking up those mountains, dude. You have to go step by step with heartfelt service to humanity, study and meditation."

Overcoming the lower self was recognizing the value beyond the self that becomes a creative agent in helping to lift all of humanity to a higher frequency.

"And there is no master who can help you, dude. The greatest master is the one least followed, the one who has mastered all his instruments … mastery of the instruments that push us forward or get in the way.

"In most cases, we give in to our appetites, our habits, all those curve balls that get thrown at us by the world of glamour out there."

"Every initiation comes with sacrifice, dude."

The Camino sure was an initiation, especially on that first path of crucifixion and the burned ground of death.

I looked at the mountain range lying ahead and felt my heart sink into my belly. This was going to be quite a climb. "It's your choice, Jake. You can still decide to take the easier, lower route. The one least traveled is the old Hospitales route."

It was going to be the Hospitales route. The hospitaliero, the hostel proprietor, who had been listening in on our conversation, recommended that we stay in Campiello for another day. The weather forecast for the next day was not good, and he strongly advised us against walking the mountain in fog and rain.

Peregrinos sometimes fail to heed the warnings and get lost in the mountains, dying of exposure when temperatures plummeted during the night.

It was a day for rest and reflection. The mountain range, blanketed in dark rain clouds loomed ahead like a covered sphinx. Above Campiello, the sky opened to an interplay of streaking white cloud paths against a backdrop of blue.

I woke frequently during the first night my heart pounding against my aching chest as fear of the unknown grasped at my throat and chest like metal chafing soft skin.

Again, fear of the unknown was rearing itself like a dragon head. Returning to a life of loneliness and loss of meaning was a bad option. If it was true that we are agents of change in the broader spectrum of humanity, why was I staring down a big black hole when even the thought of doing something meaningful for the rest of my life scared me to bits?

To become an agent of change, it was necessary to master these inner demons of the lower self. It is in our power to start a green day on a positive frequency that creates a magnetic ripple in the immediate world around.

And if I looked at my lower self, I was a moody and grumpy recluse. It was time to stop blaming others and everybody in the bad world out there for everything that had gone wrong in my life. I was solely responsible.

So, stay in the moment, my friend. Breathe deeply and in a slow rhythm. The antidote to fear was gratitude. And I was so grateful for the wonderful people I had met on the Camino: Chuck, Greta, Kristine, Andrzej and many others. I had come this far on the path, surmounting many physical and emotional challenges. I was even beginning to be grateful for past hurtful relationships.

Sacrifice on the path of crucifixion was the prelude to a higher frequency. Going through the process of pain and crossing the boundaries was opening new doors. Hurtful relationships past and present were lessons to be learned. Open your heart to compassion, Jake. Listen to your inner voice. That was easier said than done.

Darn it! There were moments when I could scream with anger at what I found were Chuck's preachy words of advice and the ease with which he seemed to be sailing through his own issues. As if guessing my thoughts, he would say:

"I'm not a master. It's just practice, practice like walking the Camino. You start with a few kilometers a day, taking a rest where needed. You go step by step and then you notice that you can do a little more and you walk a bit longer. It starts getting easier and easier as you go along. The load that once weighed a ton on your shoulder feels light and easy to carry. You start living in the moment and perceiving the wonderful world around you instead of counting the kilometers to the next destination and feeling the aches and pains in your body."

After I spent another restless night contemplating the

issue of unconditional love and compassion, my angels sent me a messenger.

He came the next morning onto the terrace while I was having breakfast, fixing me with a gaze that touched my very heart. I tried to suppress the feeling, but he wagged his tail, and pushed his wet nose against my leg or arm every time I tried to ignore him.

I called him Luke. He was a mongrel, a cross between a Scottish terrier and a golden retriever. I was sure he must have an owner, judging from his well-groomed coat. But the hospitaliero assured me that he was just another stray dog, that came to beg for food from friendly Peregrinos.

I asked the hospitaliero where the dog had come from and he just shrugged. "You can't come with me, Luke," I said. "You know that it would make my walk more difficult. I wouldn't know where to put you at night. I can't take you into any bar or café. People here in Spain seem to hate dogs. First and foremost, I can't take you back home. Can you just imagine the bureaucracy?"

Luke kept fixing me with his gaze, wagging his tail gently and then resting his head on my leg. His dark brown eyes shone with unflinching devotion.

"Unconditional love at first sight," Chuck said with a good chuckle as he took the seat next to me.

CHAPTER NINETEEN — GRATITUDE

At sunrise, the next day, Luke was waiting for me outside the front door of the Albergue, expressing his boundless, unconditional doggy joy at seeing me, running around me, and wagging his tail, while I felt guilty at not having found a way to smuggle him into my room.

The hospitaliero had sternly warned me that dogs were not allowed into the rooms for "reasons of hygiene." He even tried to persuade me to leave the dog in the village as I would have enormous difficulty finding a place to sleep in the company of a dog.

In Spain, animals belonged outside and not in the house. I had not even contemplated the problems I would encounter by taking Luke home with me.

As much as I loved Spain, I couldn't deal with the lack of kindness shown to many of the animals I had seen on the path. Dogs tied to chains all their lives on property with high walls and fencing, although it would have been no problem to let the animals roam free – worse still, kept in cages.

A lonely horse or a donkey tied to a pole on the meadow with the ground around it trampled into a dust bowel of frustration and pain.

Chuck had taught me that part of opening up to the path of enlightenment was being kind to all living beings, whether human or animal. At the same time, it was not for us to be judgmental.

"You need to know where you are. Where do you intervene to alleviate suffering and pain? Care about letting your own light shine forth in every interaction with other beings."

Leaving Campiello that morning I was happy that the rain had stopped and the weather forecast looked good for the steep climb to an elevation of 1,216 meters (3,989 feet) to the ruins of the ancient pilgrims' hospital at Hospital Fonfaraon and then to Berducedo, where we would spend the night.

Luke fixed me with his gaze as if telling me, "you are taking me with you. You won't leave me alone here, will you now?"

He was already leading the way as I took the path where Chuck and the others were waiting. We agreed to meet again at the Hospital Fonfaraon each going at his own pace but keeping each other in sight as the fog was thick and it was easy to miss the waymark. I had no intention of getting lost in the mountains again.

The mandala spider webs glistened in the morning light on the fencing along the trail that wound its way up the mountain. I concentrated on taking one step at a time, breathing heavily and feeling my heart throbbing against my chest.

Luke ran out ahead, checking out the territory, waiting for me every few minutes as if urging me on. "C'mon, it's not so difficult. Just keep going."

When I paused a little to catch my breath, he came up close nudging his nose against my hand, wagging his tail and barking softly.

My canine companion managed to instantly unlock a joy within me that I had last felt as a child. Dogs loved unconditionally. In contrast to humans, who lost their juvenile innocence with puberty at the latest, dogs could instantly change into puppy-like behavior when it came to playing with a ball or stick.

After we had climbed steadily for some hours the path ahead suddenly bathed in intense sunlight, like a gold-covered cobblestone gateway to heaven. The moon appeared like a huge lantern against the clear blue sky. Below us, the valley was still shrouded in clouds.

I had reached a point on the Camino where I felt intense gratitude. On a plateau to my left, I found a group of trees with a mound of stones left by other pilgrims. Prayers on pieces of paper were tucked between the stones.

"Gratitude is the antidote to fear," a pilgrim had written on a stone.

There were indeed so many things in my life I could be grateful for, but I had lost sight of them.

Thanksgiving had always been a part of life in ancient times. It was a ritual that paid tribute to a higher deity responsible for the cycle of seasons and a good harvest.

Yet, every day there was a reason to celebrate gratitude. It was part of Chuck's morning calibration to show and express gratitude. We took our time that morning and built a mound of stones, each stone representing an event, an incident, a memory, a person, a thing that we were intensely grateful for.

I had spent so much time in my life laying blame on others for my miserable state of mind – parents, teachers, colleagues, bosses, girlfriends, wives and the government. It was time to take responsibility for everything that had happened in my life.

All of these people had been teachers in some way or other, making me the person I was today. Each was, in truth, a reflection of the state of my own inner being.

There were stones of gratitude for my parents, grandparents, and great-grandparents, for the teachers throughout my life. I was alive, happy and healthy and enjoying a beautiful day with wonderful people on the Camino.

"Be in the moment and enjoy, Jake!" I told myself.

Events of the preceding 24 hours that I was still grateful for unfurled before my inner eye: a wonderful meal and warm bed for the night, deep conversations with fellow peregrinos, a stone with words of wisdom, a dog that had come into my life, and a wonderful walk up a mountain.

Chuck was right. It was impossible to perceive, feel and express real gratitude and at the same time be constrained by toxic emotions such as fear, anger and judgmental criticism.

Luke pushed his wet nose against my hand, looking at me with his big brown eyes and wagging his tail. "OK, Luke, I understand. We have a long way to go still."

Soon afterward we reached the ruins of Hospital Fonfaraon. It was difficult to imagine the terrible hardships the peregrinos, who,climbed these mountains in ancient times, had to face. We had good shoes and trekking clothing that protected us from the worst effects of cold and rain.

We had walked several hundred kilometers with cafés and bars catering to our every need. The peregrinos of old walked thousands of kilometers from the doorsteps of their homes, fighting hunger, disease, robbery and injury.

In those days, pilgrims would continue their journey to Santiago once their exhausted bodies had recovered in sanctuaries like these run by devoted and committed nuns who had set aside all personal needs in their practice of compassion and discipleship.

It would have been an enormous logistic task to supply the hospitals in the mountains with daily rations of food, water, medicine and, most importantly, firewood.

I felt gratitude toward those that had come before us and those that would come afte. The cycle continued in the cycle of time. The pull to Santiago was getting stronger and stronger, and I felt the excitement rise within me.

Joy came from within as I reached the top of the mountain. I shouted it out loud: "I'm happy to be alive! I want to live!"

The view from the pass at Puerto del Palo, with the Asturian mountains to the left and the rolling green hills of Galicia to the right, was spectacular.

Life had a way of rewarding those people who did not choose the easy route, took the harder one. Taking on a task that at the time we find dauntingly difficult, often turned out to be easier than we had thought.

"Yeah, Luke, the big bones that we chew on seem to be just those issues that life throws at us to deal with and to grow on."

Falling and failing was part of the process. I was amazed that I had come so far on the Camino. I had not been particularly fit, and my blistered feet had been bothering me from the first day.

Greta came to mind. I was wondering how she was doing. She was dealing with her cancer in the same way as she had learned to ride a bicycle as a child.

The bicycle was a gift from her father. She proudly took it to the playground to try it out and fell into the mud one her first attempt, making herself a laughing stock to the older children watching her.

But this strengthened her determination. Again, she fell until her knees and elbows were bleeding from all the falling. She angrily threw the bicycle onto the ground, but picked it up to try once more. This time, however, she tried balancing herself differently than before. It worked! Wobbly and shaking at first, she managed to do a full turn, on the bicycle without falling, then stopped and gasped for breath. She did a second, a third and a fourth turn, not falling once, and gaining ever greater confidence.

Neighbors who had been watching from their windows came out to congratulate her, clapping and praising her. Little Greta could ride a bicycle! She felt on top of the world.

"The lesson I learned on that day as a 4-year-old has sustained me all my life. I'm learning it again with the cancer, with the Camino, in my relationships – everything basically," she had explained to me on our trudging, walk up the Pyrenees.

I wished that I could have shared the experience of climbing the Hospital Route with her that day.

But that day my only companion was Luke, who looked at me with his ears pricked up, wagging his tail with joy.

CHAPTER TWENTY — MASS IN
A FONSAGRADA

We followed the route on a longer mountain ridge, passing the ruins of several more ancient pilgrim hospitals.

Shortly after reaching the tarred road at Lago, I noticed Chuck's familiar red backpack outside a strategically positioned bar at the roadside.

I shared my bacon-and-cheese sandwich with Luke as we discussed ways to find accommodations with a dog.

If the weather forecast was good Luke and I could sleep outdoors beneath a tree or rock outcrop. Chuck assured me that I would not have to worry about Luke.

He was an intelligent dog that would wait for me at any Albergue we chose to stay at overnight.

"He is a stray, and stray dogs know all about survival and making the best out of any situation, dude," Chuck reassured me.

Going downhill was more difficult than I had anticipated. My legs hurt and I had to walk slow. I reached the town of Berducedo long after Chuck and the others. The next day also saw a strenuous downhill route, into the valley with a lake below at La Mesa, built during the Franco dictatorship.

On the hillside to the right, derelict villas overlooked the lake. I wondered what had made people build these fine homes, only to desert them some years later.

We spent another night in the sleepy village of Grandas de Salime and learned that the fairly new houses built for the people forced to evacuate the town of Salime when the heavy hydroelectric dam was built by the dictator.

The pass of Alto del Acebo marks the boundary between Asturias and Galicia.

We reached A Fonsagrada on the afternoon of the next day.

In the Albergue near the ancient church, a group of French pilgrims were silently eating their meal, talking in sad, low voices.

The reason soon became clear to us all. The television was running without a sound, flashing news pictures of an elderly priest who had been murdered by terrorists in a French town. The world had caught up with us once again.

We all decided to attend Mass that evening in the church across the road.

The elderly priest who led the ceremony looked very similar to the clergyman who had been murdered in France that same day.

He blessed each pilgrim and made each of us repeat in

our own language:

"May the Lord guide us on our way. May he make it prosperous and healthy. May the Lord assist us and grant us companionship. May we joyfully end the way that we are trustfully on with the help of God. Amen."

He said those words with an earnestness that struck a chord within us.

Goodness, light, love and godliness define themselves in reaction to darkness. If there was any meaning in evil, it was to light the fire of love and compassion within us.

Light and darkness are one of a kind. There is no light without darkness and no darkness without light.

Hate, anger and revenge were a natural response, but to what effect? More hate and more violence, but weren't they exactly the fuel of evil?

I had seen much evil in the world during my stint as a foreign correspondent. Take Johannesburg prior to the first democratic elections in 1994. Bombs planted by right-wing extremists exploded at the international airport and in the city center. In the black townships, a war was raging between the opposition African National Congress, led by Nelson Mandela, and supporters of the Inkatha Freedom Party, backed by the apartheid security apparatus.

Burning tires at a road block. We turn around. A bullet hits the windshield of our car. We race for cover behind a wall of corrugated iron. Then we see them.

A group of Inkatha supporters with red head bands hacking a man to death in the street – cold, blind hate in their eyes. I can still hear the victims' screams, his body twitching from pain, and then no more movement.

The men stand around, share a cigarette, stare coldly at the body lying motionless in the street. Evil knows no feeling or compassion.

The Camino was generally very safe for pilgrims, nothing like during the Middle Ages, when robbers preyed on pilgrims along the route.

Chuck told us of a gruesome murder of a young American woman Denise Thiem, on the Camino in 2015 after she had apparently been lured to the property of a farmer.

But cases like that were exceptions.

"Spain is much safer than any place in the U.S.," Chuck said.

I, too, felt that in most cases the locals were courteous and more than helpful to the pilgrims. The biggest danger was at places along the Camino where pilgrims had to cross intersections or busy roads.

I felt it did no harm to remember the words of the priest and ask for protection and guidance along the route.

Before I went to bed, I made sure Luke was doing fine. I found an old blanket for him to sleep on.

"I'm right there in that Albergue hostel and you just wait for me here until the morning," I told him. Luke shoved his head into my hands as if to say: "I'll be just fine."

CHAPTER TWENTY-ONE — GALICIA

In Galicia you are going either uphill or downhill. Time seemed to have been frozen in many of the villages nestled in the valleys and mountains.

Many of the indigenous chestnut forests had made way for large-scale eucalyptus plantations over the last century. But there were efforts under way in many areas to undo the damage and to eradicate the alien trees.

Houses were built in circular form from local granite, and closely clustered together, sometimes completely isolated from the neighboring farm.

The kitchen – sometimes with a beautiful old fireplace – and animal stabling were mostly on the first floor, with the second floor housing the bedrooms and living room.

The roofing typically made of cut slate placed on sturdy chestnut beams.

Most properties had a traditional grain storage horreo raised on a plinth to protect against moisture, a protruding ledge preventing rodents from entering. The size of the horreos was an important status symbol the farmers.

Farmers could still be seen cutting the grass with a

scythe and loading the hay onto ox carts built with traditional wooden-spoked wheels used as a means of transport in Galicia since time immemorial, the high-pitched creaks of wheels on cobblestone inspiring many a musician.

In Galician legends, the oxcart was used to explain the presence of saints at certain locations. Thus, Saint Rudesind was baptized in San Miguel de Celanova, where the wheel of the cart carrying the baptismal font broke.

A conflict between the Galicians and Lusitanians on ownership of the remains of St. Eufemia was solved by tying two wild oxen to a cart. The animals kept walking until they stopped at the entrance of the city of Ourense, where the body was then taken to the cathedral.

Every so often we would pass ancient cemeteries surrounded by walls with stone crosses on them to ward off evil spirits.

Most of the traditions went back to Celtic times, and the ancient peoples spent much time contemplating on life and death. Life could be short during times of war and disease.

With these thoughts in mind, I followed the path through forest, just hearing my own feet trudging on the leafy undergrowth, and Luke panting close to me.

During those hours alone, I had taken on the habit of holding long conversations with my doggy friend. Luke would stop, look at me and move his head a little to the left and a little to the right.

"What do you think of death, Luke? You guys have a pretty short life compared with us humans, and it doesn't seem to bother you. You just take everything as it comes. Pretty cool the way you guys go about life, I must say."

I told him about my fears and a life of empty loneliness, I faced getting back home when the Camino was over. I wanted the Camino to continue like this forever, meeting interesting people, just taking every day as it came, enjoying a summer in Spain.

Luke had a habit of scouting the territory ahead and then coming back to me, wagging his tail. As we reached a clearing he stopped in his tracks, his ears pricked and the hair on his back raised, signalling to me in a low growl that there was something behind a stone wall to the right.

A head popped up ahead. It was Andrzej having his lunch of banana and orange. "Jake, buen Camino!"

Luke relaxed immediately, wagging his tail in greeting.

I had not seen Andrzej for days and was wondering about him. From his Polish and the smattering of English he had picked up on the Camino, I gathered that he had spent the past two nights outdoors, making headway by starting his walk before sunrise.

He was as cheerful as ever, offering me half of his orange. We sat down, and each talked in his own language.

We walked together for another hour until we reached a little bar and café. Chuck was there waiting for us, and he introduced a young French couple he had gotten talking to.

They were on a journey, they told us, to rediscover their Christian roots. Like many of the younger pilgrims I had met on the Camino, these young folks were on a search for a faith beyond religion and church.

They had a discussion with Chuck about Muslim extremism. "All the confrontational talk about the Muslims, the terrorist attacks, the problems with migrants in our cities, has made me think. Who are we really as French people? What do we believe in?.," Francois remarked.

Francois said he found that Christianity, Judaism and Islam all came from the same roots and had many similarities. "But why are we fighting each other like this?"

"All the big faiths have some similarities," Chuck answered. "My personal view is that God created different cultures, languages, religions, nations and ethnic groups because it's about diversity. We can only find our identity and sense of meaning in comparison and debate with our opposite. The problem arises when a lot of people with a Western mindset don't have any identity at all. That is a breeding ground for the fear, uncertainty and xenophobia that we find all over the place."

I found Francois' closing remarks quite poignant, namely that we as humans, needed a value system, some guiding beacon or inner compass that keeps us from going mad. For some it is St. James, Jesus, for others

Buddha, Allah, God, Krishna. Give everyone the freedom to choose his own God and let live."

Prior to leaving the next morning, some of the pilgrims, including the French couple, decided to walk the entire 31 kilometers (19.2 miles) to the town of Castroverde. But a thought had begun crossing my mind more frequently the past few days: to slow down more and to enjoy the Camino while it lasted. I was going to stop at the 23-kilometer (14.2 mile) marker in the town of Cadavo-Baleira which had a comfortable new Albergue.

As much as I had enjoyed the company the previous evening, I also had a responsibility to Luke. He was a dog not used to walking such long distances, and I noticed the previous day that he was not as lively as usual with a slight limp in his right hind leg. Dogs would follow their master everywhere, no matter what it took in pain and endurance. It was up to me to look after my dog.

After Luke had his meal and I my café con leche we hit the road. It took us through meadows, and old forest offering magnificent views of rolling green countryside. We stopped more frequently to enjoy the scenery. On some stages of the Camino I had been so much in a hurry to catch up with Chuck or other pilgrims I had met on the way, but now I told myself: "Jake, if you see them, you will be happy. If you don't, you will surely meet them again sometime if it is meant to be."

So many of the images on the Camino – the wild flowers, the scent of pine trees, ancient paths, skies and distant valleys were deeply etched in memory lane and could be recalled at any time. So intense were my experiences of those wonderful days, that walking had become more like a cruise than the hard act of endurance it had been during the initial stages.

There was nothing but peace and lonely contemplation during the day's walk through soft forest paths. We stopped for a lengthy break just off the path, Luke happily jumping into a little mountain spring and quenching his thirst while I bathed my feet in the cool water.

I found the Albergue in Cadavo-Baleiro to be closed, so I made my way into the town to find alternative accommodations.

I was lucky. Soon after I came to the main road a friendly lady asked me whether I needed a room, and to my surprise would allow Luke to stay with me. It was ordinary with the bathroom in the corridor but it would do just fine for us and Luke appeared more than happy to spend his first night with me indoors, with the weather forecast not looking good.

We found a rug for Luke to sleep on, and he immediately curled up into a ball with his nose tucked into his tail, to catch up on some much-needed sleep.

I was not the only guest in the house. An Austrian couple was staying in the room next door. Hans and Renate were accompanied by their golden retriever, Sonia, a trained guide dog for Hans, who was blind since birth.

They had been walking the Camino for five weeks, going short, 15 kilometer (9.3 mile) stretches and at times taking a bus when the stages between towns were too long.

I had seen parents walk the Camino with a toddler, a pilgrim in a wheelchair and an elderly lady with back problems pulling her backpack with a cart. Pilgrims, whose bodies ached, like my Polish friend Andrzej, just kept on walking step by step and kilometer by kilometer to Santiago.

But I was amazed to find a blind man walking the Camino. With encounters, such as these, I had begun to realize that there was no such thing as "I can't."

The power of the mind could defy, overcome and amazingly transform an 'I can't.' into an 'I can and I will.'

Hans and Renate had ignored all the voices around them, advising them against walking the Camino.

"Why not go on a hike in France or some other place?"

"You could stumble and hurt yourself."

"What if you got lost in the wilderness?"

"You can't take a dog, even a guide dog, to Spain. No albergue or hotel takes people with dogs."

These were like the same voices that told Greta she should not go on the Camino after cancer surgery. They were my inner demons telling me to quit my walk shortly after I had started. These were often the voices of parents and teachers telling us: "You will never be a good writer because your English is atrocious, or an entrepreneur because you can't deal with money, or excel as an artist or musician because you can't make a living out of it."

These are the voices that rob us of our dreams, of what is truly dear to us. We settle down and make a compromise that is out of line with our soul's purpose and fall into unhappiness or depression because we have forgotten how to live.

But sometimes those voices are just testing us, to see whether it really is the dream we want to follow, giving us the necessary energy and drive to pursue it because we adopt the attitude: "Now I'll show them all that I can really do it!"

Hans and Renate started planning their trip from their home base in Vienna, getting numerous rejections from the places they had planned to stay. Even hotels that had initially approved a booking in advance, turned them down upon arrival. "Sorry, our policy is no dogs allowed."

Yet they kept on going. It was one of those countless Camino miracles. Despite all the obstacles, Hans and Renate did not have to sleep outdoors once. Someone always knew someplace in town where they could stay with Sonia.

And that led to them meeting wonderful people, making new friends and thoroughly enjoying our evening – as did I – in sharing Camino experiences.

Hans, it turned out, ran a successful engineering business with several hundred employees. It was doing so well that he could take time out every year to do something special, as he called it. He had employed people of many different backgrounds and nationalities that most other companies wouldn't employ including refugees, paraplegics and people with autistic spectrum disorder (characterized by difficulty in social interaction and communication).

It was just one of the criteria that got them the job, as he put it. "I can't is not in my vocabulary."

This made his company especially innovative in developing technical solutions for construction projects all over the world.

Hans looked at me that evening, speaking in his slow, heavy Austrian accent. "You know, Jake, I've learned some things in life:

"First of all, I'm not disabled. I'm just different. If you focus on problems all the time, you will have only problems. If you focus your mind on possibilities, you open yourself up to all the opportunities that life has to offer.

"There are so many things that we worry about that can go wrong in life. But there is even a bigger possibility that everything will go just right for you. How many of the things we always worry about really happened?

"You get what you believe in. Do whatever you want to do, believing that things will work out. and they will work out for you. You must just believe that God will care for you."

CHAPTER TWENTY-TWO — LUGO

A few red-orange clouds showed up on the horizon. Contrary to the forecast, the weather looked good when Luke and I took to the road just before sunrise.

Hans and Renate were spending another day in Cadavo-Baleira. We agreed to meet again in Santiago, and when I left them I felt a little sad.

The 30-kilometer (18.6 mile) walk to the old Roman town of Lugo was a fairly easy, mainly downhill section, so I made good time in the morning.

Later in the morning we found a shady stream where Luke could have his dry bread with meat, and I had the banana and apple that I had put in my backpack the previous evening.

We were just about ready to resume our journey when our solitude was interrupted by a guttural scream that set Luke to barking incessantly, telling me this was something we needed to investigate immediately.

We rushed towards the ruins of an old building overgrown with ferns – where the noise had come from – with Luke leading the way.

Chuck and Andrzej were holding a young man to the

ground who seemed to be in an epileptic spasm, spittle running from his mouth, his eyes rolling into some void, his body trying desperately to free itself from the grip of my two friends.

A farmer with a pitch fork and several elderly women armed with brooms, sticks and pottery stood around. Chuck beckoned me to help Andrzej hold the man's kicking feet while he kept him in a headlock.

Luke had stopped his barking but kept a watchful eye on the situation, his tail ramrod, hair between the shoulder blades raised in agitation.

I noticed the sweat running from Chuck's furrowed forehead as he steadily repeated words, mantras or prayers in a mixture of languages I did not understand – apart from the very last sentence, which struck me with such fear that I almost let go of the leg still trying to kick itself free from my grip.

"Leave this soul, demon!"

The "thing" that was fighting to stay inside was screaming with great resistance. It took all our strength to keep the man pinned to the ground.

Finally there was an ear-splitting scream like a pig squeaking in a slaughter-house.

Luke barked, instantly turned around, and gave chase to some invisible force. He jumped across a rocky outcrop, turned circles came back a little toward us and then chased this "something" into the undergrowth.

Complete silence followed.

The tense body I was holding to the ground started relaxing. The young man began breathing normally, his eyes still closed as if in slumber.

During the commotion, some of the man's belongings had become scattered around him. Chuck picked up a little plastic packet and checked the contents.

"Ecstasy," he said after examining it closely.

"The problem is that these kids mix the stuff. It breaks down all the defenses and opens the gateway for the dark forces that enter through the crown or heart chakra."

We carried the young man to the nearest house in the village, where he could rest for the night and have someone offer to drive him to Lugo the next day.

Chuck assured us that he would be OK. Guardians from forces of light in another dimension were in place. The demon would not be returning.

"The man won't remember all the details, but his nervous system has been jolted with enough of a shock that I think he has learned his lesson. Others might not be so lucky."

We reached the town of Lugo later that afternoon, the temperature rising to over 30 degrees Celsius (86 Fahrenheit). Lugo, contrary to my expectations, was a disappointment at first. We kept walking past endless suburbs of bland, newly constructed apartment blocks the likes of which have spoiled so many once-beautiful Spanish towns.

The Camino took us on a cobblestone path up a

hillside with a beautiful view of the historic town center enclosed by a third century Roman wall, one of the finest Roman fortifications still intact, and a UNESCO world heritage site.

Built between 263 and 276 A.D, the wall was part of extensive fortification including a moat, against Germanic invaders from the north.

About 4 meters wide, the 2-kilometer (1.24 miles) wall is an ideal walkway for visitors, with five of the 10 gates dating from Roman times. Just inside the wall is St. Mary's Cathedral, our first destination.

The oldest part of the cathedral dates back to 1129 A.D, originally constructed as a Romanesque-Gothic temple. At the front, two bell towers sandwich a triple-arched main block including vertical columns.

It is positioned at St. James Gate, one of the main gateways of medieval pilgrims heading out of Lugo toward Santiago de Compostela.

On a more recent, Baroque square at the rear the Palacio Episcopal faces the cathedral. As we entered the cathedral, we were at first struck by its darkness, which opened up to the bright light of the main altar with its elaborate gold decorations. If this weren't enough the area behind the altar was even more stunning.

I had to sit down to gather my senses as I contemplated the awesome structure, inspired by – the Mother Goddess, illuminating light, love and a serene calmness.

I was overwhelmed by the interplay of darkness and

light, in the painting which depicted the Virgin Mary at the temple where she was taken at the age of 13 to be educated until she became the mother of Jesus. In another section was a reliquary bust of St. John the Baptist and the Lamb of God in the middle.

St. James was depicted in various paintings and sculptures with emphasis on different spiritual characteristics: the guardian, the serene master, the leader, the mentor and he who smiles within like a modern-day star bewildered by all the media attention.

The images melted into each other, almost as if his features were coming alive, and as I felt waves of cold and warm air hit me from behind.

I fled out into the open square to catch my breath and align my senses. It was all just too much. I felt dizzy and passed out.

I woke up some time later as Chuck poured half a bottle of cold water over my head. Luke licked my face.

"You need to rest, my friend – been a bit much for a day," he said.

I felt my hard-beating pulse and a sharp pain in my chest. "I think I'm having a heart attack!" I moaned.

"No, you're not," Chuck said sharply. "Pull yourself together, man. Your dog is getting all worried."

We found a place to stay near the cathedral with a courtyard at the rear with an enclosure where Luke could sleep for the night. There was no talking with the innkeeper. Dogs were not allowed inside.

CHAPTER TWENTY-THREE — REJUVENATION

"Remain humble on the path, or the path will humble you."

The words of warning, Claire had given me before I set out on my pilgrimage took on much more meaning that day.

The Camino was so much more than a physical endeavor. My body easily accomplished the 30-kilometer walk to Lugo from Cadavo-Baleira. The typical morning cramps and muscle aches during the first weeks of my walk were no more. Now my body craved for the steady rhythm I had found within me.

Whereas each step with a heavy backpack had triggered a pain somewhere, I now felt a lightness of being and physical fitness that made walking up a mountain but a small challenge.

I tried to explain my collapse outside the cathedral with my having gone too fast in the midday sun, when most Spaniards are indoors for a siesta. Some of them shake their heads in disbelief at the ignorant peregrinos risking a heat stroke.

But I had walked more strenuous stages the days

before in similar heat. I was probably much fitter than most people after having walked my good 20-25-kilometers (12.42-15.5 miles) each day for the previous three weeks.

My body was having to deal with emotions that had come to the surface and thrown me to the ground to once again learn humility.

I was not as far down the road as I had thought. As Chuck, would say: "When you think you know it, life comes around the corner to give you a whack so that you can learn the next lesson."

I spent the next several days in Chuck's house in the mountains near Lugo. It was one of the typical Galician stone houses, situated on a mountain top with a breathtaking view of the surrounding countryside.

On its southside, he had built a patio that extended over a cliff. While the ground floor was kept in typical Galician style and had a fireplace and kitchen, the upper floor was one big room with two bedrooms extending to the rear. A circular glass dome in the middle filled the room with light. The walls were decorated with Indian landscape art, depicting the Arizona desert and the red cliffs of Sedona.

Chuck had bought the place, a former cattle shed, several years ago, renovating it with the help of local craftsman. It came with several acres of land and its own water supply. Electricity was supplied by solar panels on the roof of the adjacent shed.

"You don't have to pose the question, dude," Chuck said after showing me around the house. "Why don't I spend all my time here, painting, reading, writing, gardening – all the things I really enjoy doing?

"I kind of enjoy my alone time here, dude. But it's a selfish lifestyle to do it all the time. It gets lonely, and the Camino has given me so much that I need to give something back. Like this time: I spent some weeks as a hospitaliero in an Albergue, just before we met, in fact.

"We need to find that passion, the fire within us, that drives our creative force. Happiness is not just fate but the outcome of hard work and changing bad habits into good ones.

"Once you do that, you will have the energy to apply your full potential to making a positive contribution to the world at large with your individual talent. When we find that groove, everything falls into place. I did not find this place. It found me and through it I met some wonderful people in this area who are very good friends now.

"Happiness grows with dedication to your lifelong dream, your passion and becoming your full self. That will catapult you forward. Of course, we have setbacks, down periods. But that is life, for God's sake – having to deal with these ebbs and flows.

"When we do something we love and are passionate about, there is a resonance with the world. Start with something small that is really important to you and let the joy and the happiness in going about it spread to the world."

It sounded so simple. But when I thought about my passion, I just saw a void. I had felt that passion at times in my life, filing a news story ahead of the competition and seeing my byline on the front pages of newspapers around the globe. I had firmly believed I was on a mission to change the world by digging in the muck and revealing the truth behind the empty words and lies of those in power.

Over the years, I had become cynical, realizing that I would not change anything by writing another news story. Having a byline on a story was noticed only in the echo chamber of fellow journalists and my own ego.

The media were business enterprises vying for the attention of listeners and readers. The higher the circulation, the higher the advertising revenue. And the only way of getting the attention of readers was through negative and racy headlines.

The human mind worked that way. Attention was paid mostly to the negative, not the positive. If the story was not in the political arena, attention was focused on famous figures in entertainment, some of them having bad behavior as their only claim to fame.

Yes, Chuck was right. I had to find my groove and I was still a very long way from finding the passion that could reignite the fire within me.

I slept most of the next night and day. Luke seemed content sleeping at my bedside. Chuck did take him out for walks, I later found out, introducing him to the many local dogs and cats.

I felt a lot better after the third day. "You've been pushing yourself too hard," Chuck said.

"Sometimes you have to allow things that come from deep inside to just develop at their own pace and rhythm. Like a seed growing into a plant, not asking about the next rain. It comes anyway, as every season has its time.

"You need real patience for matters of the heart to grow to fruition. Love and accept those unresolved questions that come. They are like locked rooms that need their time to find the keys. Immerse yourself into those questions and over time you will start growing into the answers."

Our conversation was interrupted by a knock on the door. It was Carlos and his wife, Alesia, who greeted Chuck with exuberant exclamations, hugs and kisses. We were invited to a fiesta in the village that evening.

Carlos played the guitar and sang traditional Galician songs, melancholy stories about sad fishermen who went out to sea and never returned. But there were also vibrant rhythmic songs about the birth of a child or an abundant harvest that could enkindle joyful dancing.

Several of the townsfolk joined in with the singing. A toothless, elderly granny gathered the other women into an inner circle while the men formed an outer circle for a traditional dance. Then all of us joined in, clapping and dancing to the rhythm.

Even Luke was having fun, having befriended a group of village dogs that were playfully chasing each other.

I could hardly remember having had such fun partying with a group of people. It was a celebration of the community spirit, an ancient bond that came from the realization that an individual could not survive alone. A child was raised by the village, the frail and sick were a responsibility for all. Building a barn, a house or bringing in the harvest could only be done as a community.

Modern man seemed to have lost something along the way, I thought. He lived in the illusion that he could make it alone in the world, forgetting that his whole being was forged from early childhood as a member of a specific group, family, tribe or village. We adopt the mannerisms, thoughts, ideas and even dress codes of the people we are surrounded with.

Despite the influence of uniform pop-culture, it amazed me how the different cultures on the Iberian Peninsular placed great emphasis on preserving their unique traditions. I had met Basques, Asturians and Galicians who were proud of their ancestry, deeply rooting them to the land they lived on.

But this world was under threat. I noticed that most of the people around us were elderly. There was a massive exodus of the younger people to other countries and the big cities.

Spain, like many of the southern European countries, had been suffering for years from high youth unemployment. Indeed, we had walked through many a deserted village with once beautiful, old stone houses and stately rural farmsteads crumbling into mounds of rubble and weeds.

"You can dwell in sadness on what was and will never come back, or embrace the new avenues of opportunity that comes your way. It's a pity that most of us don't see these opportunities, because our minds are fogged by the veil of the past," Chuck said to me as I again lamented the state of the world.

As our remaining time together grew short, I noticed that Chuck was becoming more impatient with my lamentations. He felt an inner mission to leave a mark on me that would keep me walking the path, long after I had finished walking the Camino.

The lessons I was learning on the Camino were so intense and life-changing that they threw me into a dizzy spin. It would take me many weeks and months to fully digest the transitions that were happening on a deep, subconscious level.

I wanted a clear answer to how I was going to live the remaining years of my life. I felt the answer so palpably close and then eluding my grasp.

Chuck continued to reassure me that the answer would come in its own time. But I was getting impatient and irritable with myself.

"You really need to forgive yourself, dude. Accept yourself as you are at this moment in time. Show gratitude to your inner child, what has come all this way. There is nothing pushing you to accomplish something within a certain time frame.

"Remember that you have all the time in the world and no time to lose, dude. Free your mind of all thought."

There he was again, Chuck, the master who knew it all, preaching to me.

Luke seemed to guess my thoughts. He looked at me long and hard, his brown eyes touching a spot in my heart that made me soften. What this dog was teaching me was unconditional love. He had decided on the spur of the moment to follow me and stay at my side, and I thanked the guardian angels that had sent him to guide me on that last stretch of the Camino, which was becoming a great emotional rather than physical challenge.

Chuck and I spent our last evening together that day. I was sad about losing my teacher, companion and friend. He told me there were urgent things he had to attend to. I didn't ask an further.

Santiago was around the corner, less than a week away, and now Chuck was going AWOL on me. I was disappointed. The bond between us had grown deep and I really wanted to share that moment of glory walking into the cathedral with him.

"Savor that moment alone. Absorb it with all your thoughts, energy and inner wisdom," he told me as we parted.

"We'll see each other again, dude."

That was it. We would remain in touch. Yeah, I thought. As soon as I was gone, I would be forgotten. I was blaming myself. Had I been too intense, too selfish abusing him as a teacher, therapist, coach, guide and companion?

As I continued my Camino the next morning, my mind went back to the many wonderful evenings we had shared, philosophizing about life, spirit and the world we lived in.

"You can dwell in sadness on what was and will never come back, or embrace the new avenues of opportunity that comes your way," I recalled him saying.

Luke raced ahead, and in the distance the chiming of a church bell that reverberated through the forest like an echo touching my heart strings.

I mulled over the last conversations I had had with Chuck. I had been focused on using willpower to find answers to life's big questions. And it was "wanting" to that had pushed me into exhaustion.

"Look at it like walking along a forest path," Chuck had said. "You can see the forest as a piece of property you would like to own, with timber you might want to sell. The relationship is based on plans, money, worries and concerns.

"If you don't want anything from that tree or forest and just look at it without possessiveness, inhaling its fresh aroma, enjoying the greenery, then you accept the beauty of the forest as it is.

"But if you approach something with the intention of wanting something from it, be it a thing or a human being, you will miss its essence.

"At the moment you release intention, you start seeing, and your soul reaches out to unconditional love. You see the beauty that is: People are no longer distorted reflections of your needs. Young or old, male or female, friendly or unfriendly are no longer categories. Everything, everybody has a soul beauty of its own."

Instead of taking the easier route to Melide, where the Camino Primitivo merged with the main Camino Frances, I decided to take the longer walk to the monastery at Sobrado dos Monxes.

The two-day walk along narrow forest paths and through isolated villages was slow and leisurely. It was overcast and rainy. Luke didn't seem bothered by the weather, remaining cheerful, despite having to shake himself frequently to rid his coat of the drenching water.

The monastery towers were visible from afar, and I wondered if Santiago would look much the same. As we walked down the hillside, the clouds opened, illuminating the bell towers.

Sobrado monastery dates back to the year 952 and was run by Cistercian monks from the 12th century until it was forcibly closed by the government in 1835, after which the buildings fell into decay. However, Cistercian monks began reconstruction in 1954, and in 1966 a new monastic community was formed that is still active. An Albergue is situated in the former stables.

A jovial workman wearing overalls and a straw hat met us at the gate. The Albergue was filling up fast as dozens of pilgrims from the coastal route were streaming in. He was very helpful in giving me an address in town where a friendly middle-aged couple was only too happy to provide Luke and me with a bed for the night. The lady of the house insisted that Luke would be safe with her and that I should enjoy Mass in the monastery that evening.

It was a scene that was beyond time and space, I felt

myself catapulted back to the 11th century. The monks, all dressed in white robes, entered the chapel walking in single file. I recognized the "workman", who had greeted us at the gate as one of the monks. They were of different nationalities and ages, their singing echoed through the ancient chamber. The sermon was by an elderly monk with intense, dark eyebrows contrasting with his white hair.

He spoke in slow, clear Spanish, of Jesus' Sermon on the Mount. In our rush and preoccupation with material needs, there was a warning not to forget the needs of the soul, to trust what God expected from us, and to serve what was far greater than the self.

It reminded me of word by my mentor Chuck, shortly after we had met. There are problems and there are difficulties, he had said. Most of the time we are dealing with difficulties, not problems.

So many times, the path had taught me to trust. On the many occasions, I had strayed far off the marked path, someone, would appear as if from nowhere, to show me where to go.

The day before, an elderly granny had taken pity on me. Taking me by the hand, she led me some distance through a rundown village until I finally saw the waymark.

I recalled the day when I was about to throw in the towel. Chuck came into my life at precisely the moment I had decided to give up. So, I concluded – God wanted me to learn my lessons on the Camino.

Every day on the Camino it was the same lesson:

taking one step at a time, being in the moment with the moment defining the future, don't look back and don't look at the distance you have to walk.

In the monastery, I again found a statue of the Mother, with features like those in a work of art by Picasso, narrow, expressive facial features with a hidden message for people willing to contemplate, opening their heart and mind.

It was a face beyond any distortion, transcending time and space.

The goddess showed herself in many shapes and forms. I imagined the sculptor, many hundreds of years ago, contemplating the piece of rock, seeing her image in stone and then chipping away bit by bit until she was there for all the world to see.

Countless generations of pilgrims would be inspired by her and find answers. Prayer could be pleadingly mundane in always wanting something – an answer, a resolution to a problem at hand, an instant miracle.

The power of prayer was beyond words, beyond arrogant and juvenile expectations of having an immediate need to be fulfilled.

The mystery was really in the seeking, in the humble recognition that we were all children of God and should say "yes" to the bigger matrix that went far beyond individual wants and needs.

The challenge was to pray for the wisdom to stay the path in gratitude, and to transcend the level of self-inflicted pain of constant concerns and wants.

CHAPTER TWENTY-FOUR — GRETA

Spending five weeks on solitary paths in rugged countryside and then reaching the bustling city life of Arzua was like being hit by a jarring heavy-metal band after having become accustomed to the sounds of birdsong, wind and the rustling of leaves in eucalyptus, pine and oak forests.

Keeping my "ear to the ground" had received a whole new meaning on the Camino Primitivo. This was why an ancient legend told us that Mary conceived Jesus through the ear – the organ closest to BEING and original sound.

I was learning to listen to my own breathing, and hearing my own heartbeat again. Listening in silence to nature, a bird sing, a cricket chirp, the distant bleating of a sheep or the chiming of a cow bell was more than just becoming aware. It opened a space and beyond that, the precious silence of within.

It was a relatively short walk of 22 kilometers (13.6 miles) from Sobrado dos Monxes to Arzua, where the three main Camino routes conjoined into the main artery, only 40 kilometers (24.85 miles) from Santiago.

I recalled the singing and meditation with the monks in Sobrado the night before. What had made these men, each of them very different, decide to withdraw from the world and to spend the rest of their lives behind the walls of an ancient monastery?

They had left a lasting impression on the group of pilgrims listening to their prayers and softly sung hymns. A part of me, was impressed and awed by the courage to leave forever the magnetic pull of a world of distraction, sexual desire and material needs.

Arzua, the largest town before Santiago, contrasted with Sobrado with its brash southern European vibrancy.

Large crowds of young pilgrims occupied the main Albergues, talking and singing. Day tourists poured out of buses to walk short stretches of the Camino Frances. School classes were being disciplined by their teachers. The familiar sound of Spanish television at full volume blared from the patios of restaurants.

Luke pressed himself close to my legs, his body on alert, sniffing the ground suspiciously and pricking his ears at every unaccustomed noise. "Don't worry, Luke. We will find a place to stay and it won't be in one of these crowded and noisy Albergues. They wouldn't want us anyway," I said, more to myself than to Luke, who always seemed to tell me: "Don't worry, everything will be just fine."

Then, I noticed a familiar blonde, confidently striding into a nearby restaurant. "Greta!" I was overjoyed at seeing a familiar face after so many days.

We fell into each other's arms like close family members who had not seen each other for years. Greta instantly fell in love with my companion Luke. There was so much we had to share.

I was thankfully surprised at how well she was doing. Her body was well tanned. She had exchanged her heavy hiking boots for light hiking sandals that were much easier on her feet. The pained look in her eyes had given way to a confident clarity. Greta had found herself on the Camino.

"I cheated some of the way in case you are wondering how I've made it so far," she said with a coquettish smile. "I took the bus for some of the way."

After we had separated in Puente la Reina, Greta had chosen to continue on the Camino Frances, "walking my path in my own time and at my own pace," avoiding, as she put it, "the distractions from other pilgrims in the Albergues," by spending her nights in simple hotels, small privately-run hostels and guesthouses, withdrawing behind dark sunglasses under a huge straw hat.

Walking alone on the Camino is a path of self-discovery and deep, inner reflection. It is when a person is alone in unknown territory that demons lurk and angels guide – a period of probation, trial and temptation.

There comes the discovery that walking in loneliness is a gift revealing the soul's purpose.

I recounted my walk on the Primitivo until leaving Chuck at his house. I expressed my disappointment at the three of us being unable to share that evening together in Arzua.

"It was meant to be that way," she said.

While she was talking, I wondered about the new Greta.

This was a Greta who was upbeat, who listened intently without interrupting, was more reflective and physically of little resemblance to the woman who had been burdened by a heavy backpack and literally dragged herself forward with every step.

Her movements were nimble, relaxed, and she seemed very much at ease with herself.

"What happened to you?" I asked, complimenting her and then telling her how I had perceived her.

"You were feeling miserable about yourself and about life. Your outbursts of temper and constant bickering was irritating and a part of me was relieved when you went your own way," I admitted.

"Yes, you are right," she said. "I was not good company and I'm sorry for that."

She went on to tell me her story.

In what proved to be a test of her willpower Greta fell ill with food poisoning soon after she had left us, and had to spend two days shuttling between a bed and bathroom.

Mentally and physically at the lowest point of her Camino, she nevertheless decided to take a short 12 kilometer walk to the next village, where she could take a bus to Burgos and from there to Bilbao and a flight back home.

Reaching the village exhausted, she headed for the courtyard of a church. While washing her dusty face with tap water, she noticed that the door of the church was open. Churches in the smaller towns and villages in Spain were locked on most days, much to the chagrin of pilgrims wishing to take a peek inside or to stop for a moment of contemplation or prayer.

Following an impulse, she entered the church, her eyes taking some time to get accustomed to the darkness. Looking around, she noticed a priest in the far corner, who lit a candle and walked toward her, greeting her with a friendly smile.

He was a small man with thick white hair and facial features that made it difficult to even estimate his age. He was old, but at the same time young in his bearing and demeanor.

After placing a candle in her hand, the priest led Greta to the altar on the center of which a silver cross was positioned. Then he placed a match in Greta's hand, beckoning her to light the candle and to place it in front of the cross.

What happened next Greta described as an experience that "knocked me off my feet." The priest steadied her, until she regained her composure, and she felt a warm gust of air blowing into her face and a surge of energy rising in her body.

The priest blessed her, praying for protection in all spheres and dimensions, gesturing both upward and downward and then said in parting that she would find the answer she was looking for in the Cathedral of Santiago de Compostela.

She stayed in a privately-run hostel that night and got talking to her host, a retired Belgian teacher named Jacques.

"Who is that friendly old priest, I met in the church today?" she asked him.

"Old priest? Are you sure?" Jacques replied.

"There is no old priest in the village. We have only a young Polish priest who comes from the nearest town once a month to give Mass. And the church is never open. It is only open on one Sunday a month for Mass."

"Are you really sure, you are talking about our village?" Jacques asked, taking off his glasses and cleaning them carefully with his handkerchief and looking at Greta in a way that questioned her sense of reality.

At that point in our conversation, Greta paused. I stopped her from trying to find the right words. Deeply spiritual experiences were beyond words.

It was like trying to replicate a picture related by a stranger and missing all the wonderful details like the shades of light falling on blades of grass, the hue of the sky, the nuances of a facial expression and the composition of objects at a certain angle.

CHAPTER TWENTY-FIVE — SANTIAGO

It seemed the closer we got to Santiago, the bigger the crowds and the faster the walk.

We were on the path before dawn, and already it was filling up with people.

There were those still fresh from starting their walk in Sarria in order to obtain the "Compostela", the certificate for having walked at least 100 kilometres on foot. And, there were limping and aching peregrinos, who were forcing the last ounce of energy from their bodies to make it to Santiago.

Greta, walking next to me, repeated her mantra, which became mine: "I'm walking my own pace. I'm walking my own rhythm. Go slow, go steady."

She was forced to go slowly, because her right knee hurt.

"I was going so well, and now this has to happen to me, so close to Santiago!"

We saw this as a sign from heaven that we needed to enjoy the last two days before Santiago and not to be drawn into the energy of those moving past us with great haste.

It was only 40-kilometers (24.85 miles) to Santiago and after spending the night in Pedrouzo we would reach the Cathedral for the pilgrims' Mass the next day.

I had done little mindful walking on the Camino. Often my thoughts would wander, or I would lose my way, then concentrate again on finding the next yellow waymark or my mind would simply enter a realm of autonomous emptiness.

Walking with Greta that day taught me that mindful walking was a wonderful way to bring body and mind together. Every step took us closer to home – not the destination of Santiago, but the connection with the inner mind and body in the here-and-now.

Finding an inner connection to feelings in the here-and-now through conscious breathing with every step took practice.

It was not by avoiding the people who greeted us with a friendly "buen camino!" but by being fully aware of the world around you, the smells, the sounds, the wind and the sunshine.

The physical perception of walking, was feeling the body, the sensation of the feet touching the ground, and the rising and falling energy within the body with every inhalation and exhalation.

Placing every foot mindfully on this holy path was very different than just walking. Stopping to take a break, concentrating again on breathing and aligning the center of the head with the universe and the soles of the feet with the Earth, opened the body up to a strong wave of energy, rising and withdrawing like a tide.

In autonomous mode, we walk with an objective in mind: getting from A to B as fast as possible. In mindful walking we turn all our attention to the sensation of walking and breathing, bringing the mind out of its erratic and troubled dance between the past and the future.

It was about creating a space of tranquility in a sea of turbulence, so that the present moment could be enjoyed to the fullest.

We laughed at the sky, touched the branches of the eucalyptus trees, smelled the aroma, stretched out our backs on a meadow with sheep bleating around us and Luke snuggling between us.

It was movement and stillness at the same time, with all obstacles and running thoughts momentarily banished from the mind.

Santiago, appeared to us on the hill known as Monte Gozo as the morning mist started clearing. With none of the today's modern buildings obstructing the view of the cathedral as the city's focal point, the pilgrims of old must have been overwhelmed at finally reaching their destination.

In slow-motion step by step we followed the way marks embedded in the sidewalks that guided us all the way to the historic city center and the cathedral.

We went through the dark passageway leading to the Praza do Obradoiro, and then we entered the square, with the cathedral presenting itself in all its splendor.

Greta was overcome by emotion, tears streaming down her cheeks. We looked around and discovered a familiar face in the crowd. Andrzej, our Polish friend, whom I had not seen for days, had made it before us. We hugged, we smiled, we laughed.

And then another familiar face – Chuck.

"Just had to come to check you guys out."

We made it just in time for the midday pilgrims' Mass, Chuck said in leading the way. It was one of those special occasions when the Compostela Botafumeiro, the famous giant thurible, was swung by eight red-robed tiraboleiros through the transept, spreading thick clouds of incense.

The hymn, sung by a nun, was of such clarity and intensity that it moved me to wipe away a tear. After years in which I had closeted the voice of my heart with intellectual and rational thought the barrier had finally fallen.

God could not be explained. He could only be felt.

CHAPTER TWENTY-SIX — THE CATHEDRAL

The Cathedral of Santiago is one of the world's great masterpieces of art, built, rebuilt, extended and refined by architects, sculptors, stone masons and painters over the centuries.

Every small detail and symbol is filled with a mystery that is beyond time, speaking to the heart of a person in the 21st century just as it did to the pilgrims of old.

The final destination of the pilgrims is the crypt below the main altar with the relics of St. James in a silver reliquary in the remnants of the 9th century church.

It's an old tradition for pilgrims waiting in line to climb up the stairs behind the altar to embrace the Baroque statue of St. James.

Upon exiting the crypt, you encounter nine side chapels, each uniquely decorated and providing space for contemplation.

We spent hours meditating, observing and simply enjoying the atmosphere inside the cathedral.

It radiates the joy of pilgrims having finally reached

their destination. There is an almost complete absence of depictions of cruelty or punishment, the images concentrating on the joyful message of abundance, salvation and gratitude instead.

Greta looked at me.

"Remember, shortly after we met I complained to you about Christianity and all its emphasis on suffering and the Crucifixion. Now I understand. Isn't it that pain and joy that are a part of the same coin?"

Over the cathedral's Puerta Santa entrance, St. James looks down gently on the pilgrims below, almost as if saying:

"Happy, you made it, dude. Welcome home."

The central figure at the Portico de la Gloria is considered one of the finest pieces of medieval sculptures, depicting the resurrected Christ with outstretched arms as if lovingly embracing humanity.

I well remember a conversation with Chuck in Puente la Reina the resurrection symbolizing the mystical rebirth of the soul to a raised consciousness.

The message has been distorted for centuries. We are not destined to live a life bearing our cross in pain and suffering, with salvation coming in the hereafter.

Resurrection is about the here and now. It is the awakening of soul, discovering that God within so that the greatness can shine forth its light into the world.

Walking the Camino is analogous of the Easter story, starting with the pure physical challenge on the path of

Crucifixion, followed by the walk of loneliness through the valley of death and letting go of old wounds and attachments as the necessary precondition for renewal and resurrection.

Greta's complaint was that most of practiced Christian religion had gotten stuck in the ritualization of the pain and suffering, symbolized by the cross, and forgotten the central message of joy and happiness in the resurrection.

And as Greta opened her heart, the cathedral spoke to her through the Platerias façade at the south portal. I will summarize in her own words, the message.

"All this time I had rejected God as a male figure of control, anger and manipulation sowing the seeds of fear.

"Here I finally find a God, realigning the male aspect with his heart and gently guiding him on that one crucial step into an unknown world. And then there is God treating Eve, the woman, on equal terms. She is not regarded as part of the male, but seen as a person in her own right.

"God speaks directly to the heart, not through the words of some messenger like a priest or church.

"Everything has meaning and is good. No more fear. I am blessed, just happy."

The gentle gaze and the loving gestures depicted by the unknown artist all fused into the central message of a declaration of love to humanity.

Man and woman are portrayed as equal images of God, called upon to live life to the fullest, the heart and mind being equal parts within them.

Pilgrims who have reached Santiago know of that meeting of hearts, the exchange of greetings, the close encounters between pilgrims, strangers at first and then close confidantes on the path, sharing deep experiences, food and drink.

Greta, Chuck and I had shared so much. We had met, parted and then met again. We recollected our physical and emotional pains along the way, the moments of joy and intense debates over a glass of wine in the evenings.

We felt the joy of having reached our destination and the sadness of having to say goodbye to each other. Greta would be taking a flight back to Stockholm the next day. Chuck would be returning to his finca. We might remain in touch or never see each other again.

I would continue my walk the next day to Muxia and on to the "end of the world" at Cape Finisterre. I needed more time to digest my experiences, to recollect and to prepare for a new life back home. And I had to figure out a way to take, Luke, with me.

The Camino was a fast-track course in life and there were many more lessons to be learned.

"Just keep on walking, dude. You are capable of more than you think," Chuck said as we parted – the same words as when we first met in Sarrance, France.

Relationships – in whatever form – that we begin or end close a chapter. We need to be grateful to the people who are a blessing in our lives and let go of those who have a toxic influence.

Chuck had been an excellent teacher and mentor on the path. With Greta I had shared deep emotional and spiritual feelings. Had we met at a different time and in a different place, our relationship could have become more. But on the Camino, this would have distracted from the inner soul searching and the precious insights won during those walks alone.

Love was often confused with sexuality, and we both realized that anything beyond a Camino bond would have led to complications that neither of us could have dealt with at the time.

I was going to keep on walking to Finisterre to deal with my loneliness, just happy to have Luke at my side, who seemed only too happy to leave the bustling city.

The other side of Santiago is that of places overrun by tourists with hundreds of souvenir shops selling Camino paraphernalia, and noisy open-air restaurants and bars.

I had decided to take the route via the seaside town of Muxia to Cape Finisterre. The route predates Christianity, the Celts having believed it to be place where the sun died and the worlds of the dead and the living came closer, with a thin line separating death, resurrection and rebirth.

I remembered Chuck's words on the Camino when we discussed the mythology of the field of starts. Walking to Finisterre was walking from the old life, the past in the West, to a new, cleansed future in the East.

Cape Finisterre was a magical place dedicated to the dying sun. The ancient Celts made offerings and sacrifices to please the gods. The coastline between Cape Finisterre and Muxia is strewn with shipwrecks and called the Costa da Morte, or the Coast of Death. Many a fisherman over the ages failed to return from a rough night at sea.

Deeply rooted in ancient traditions, this was a part of Spain that long resisted conversion to Christianity until, it is said, the Virgin Mary appeared along the Muxia coastline in a stone boat. The Nosa Senora da Barca church was built on a site where one of the stones is the shaped like the bow of a ship.

True or not, the stones at Muxia are said to have magical powers and were used by the Celts for various love and healing rituals.

It was the goddess Celt, the mother of all Galician Celts, who lay hidden in the sacred stones at Muxia.

Celt or Mary. She was the mother who changed shape and form, beyond time and space.

Those last days spent along the beautiful beaches of Muxia remain frozen in memory, like the boundless joy of Luke chasing a stick into the crashing waves.

The invisible can only be perceived when you search for the light within, the seeds of love and light grow and become aware of those magical moments when creation reveals its language.

I paused on a wooden bridge on the magically beautiful coastline. Sunrays penetrated the clouds, illuminating the water. A fish swam within reach, moving on its side to showcase its wonderful silver belly in the reflecting light.

And all that lives on the Earth was created out of pure joy in the love of life.

For me the Camino was no magical moment of enlightenment. Too rich were the many small enlightenments along the way, the cognizance that letting go and allowing the Universe or God to guide the way, was the key.

Recognizing God comes from self-recognition, full self-acceptance and the love of the God within.

The path is hard, rugged, steep, easy, ugly and beautiful. We have moments of happiness and moments of sadness. Inner turmoil is followed by peace of mind. Hours of loneliness and inner reflection are just as much a part of the Camino as the friendships, the camaraderie and chance meetings with exceptional people.

From my fellow peregrinos I learned that happiness is a state of mind, the simple acceptance of life's ebb and flow, the ability to rise to the occasion in just going step by step.

Life is not something that just happens – we are an integral part of it, and everything that happens to us is life's response to our own thoughts, emotions and actions.

I passed a café along the way into Cap Finisterre with a special message on a headstone:

"The real Camino starts at the end."

On my final day of the Camino I watched the sun set

from the lighthouse at Cap Finisterre. From the way marker zero on the ragged, towering cliffs, there was a lovely view toward the endless horizon across the sea. No beginning and no end.

One journey ends and a new journey begins.

CHAPTER TWENTY-SEVEN — EPILOGUE

It's been more than a year since the walk. Memories are deeply etched in my mind. I hear the voices of the locals wishing "buen Camino!", see the jovial, sunburned faces of those that showed me the way toward Santiago, each time I missed a waymark.

I remember the many pilgrims I shared experiences with and the close bonds and friendships that grew.

The smell of fresh herbs along the mountain paths of the Pyrenees still fills my nostrils. The tinkle of cow bells in the valleys. The cool wind blowing against my face from the Bay of Biscay is recalled in an instant.

There is Chuck's deep American drawl, the images of St. James and the Madonna in the many portraits and statues along the way.

A fire is crackling in the fireplace at my home back in Ireland. Luke is on the sofa, snoring contentedly. Bringing him was less of a problem than I had thought. Spain and Ireland are both members of the European Union, which made things so much easier. I had to have Luke vaccinated against rabies and microchipped so that he could fly back home with me.

Friends and family members tell me that I am a different person, since I came back from the Camino.

I feel a different meaning and purpose in the spiritual, something far beyond what conventional theology has taught over the centuries with a head mind, the voice of the heart from the mystics of old, having been silenced for so long.

We come into this world as an individual with a deep inhalation and leave this world with a deep exhalation. The truth is within and can only be discovered from within.

I found a God calling through the heart, whispering to me through the wind in the trees, speaking to me in my dreams, looking at me with unconditional love through the eyes of Luke, sending me an answer through the timeless, soft smile of an ancient Madonna sculpture.

We live life for a purpose – a dream seeking to find expression. Nothing is coincidental. We need to discover – what makes us unique as co-creators on the ever growing spiral of the evolution of consciousness.

Life is a cycle of walking through crucifixion and the valley of death, and finding rebirth through resurrection.

It is precisely during those periods of loneliness and desolation, with a Jesus crying out on the cross: "Father why hast though forsaken me?" that we move forward into a raised consciousness.

I yearn for those long conversations with my good friend Chuck. As much as our meeting was coincidental, so mysterious was his disappearance. After repeated unanswered e-mails, letters and non-returned calls, I feared the worst. I finally managed to get hold of someone in his village on the phone who spoke some English.

Everyone in the village knew Chuck. A visiting student granddaughter of one of the village elders told me that he had sold his finca to a French couple.

There were rumors going around. Chuck was a constant topic of conversation. A story went, he had gone back to the home of his Indian ancestors in the Arizona desert.

Another was that he had decided to become a monk in a remote mountain monastery in the Basque region. One villager purportedly heard a rumor that Chuck's old life as an intelligence agent had caught up with him after strangers with Eastern European accents had come to the village looking for him.

There was also the version that he had become terminally ill and died, which I refused to believe. Chuck was a drifter, a mover who embraced change.

I searched the Internet for hours, hoping to find some clue to his whereabouts. We live in an age where a human being simply does not disappear without leaving an electronic footprint.

In retrospect, I realized that in the many of our long conversations, Chuck had revealed very little of that part of his life prior to moving to Spain. It was not that he had been hiding something but I was too self-indulgent with my own issues to have delved into asking more about him.

Who was he really? Was his name really Chuck Jones? It sounded too common a name and had he adopted a new identity for reasons we didn't know?

Greta and I remain good friends and frequently do Skype calls. She recently spent a weekend, and we had a lovely time reminiscing about the Camino.

She is happy to indulge in those fond memories but just as adamant that "it is something I will never do again."

Greta is cancer-free, and has found a new purpose as a yoga teacher in her own therapy studio on the outskirts of Stockholm. She finally convinced me to stop searching for Chuck.

"If he wants to be found, he would know where to find us. He will have his reasons for having gone underground. I miss him too – very much," she said, her voice faltering, before she caught herself.

"He will be back, I'm sure."

Every so often I feel a strong urge, a deep yearning to pick up my backpack once again, and to head for the Camino, hearing that voice etched deep in my heart like a lasting clarion call:

"Just keep on walking, dude."

.